Spectacular, Spectacular!

Für Constanze

Tina xx

19. 01. 2012

"Spectacular, Spectacular!"

stories & poems by
Creative Writing Group of the
Anglistische Seminar Heidelberg

edited by
Marina Machauer
Tina F. Hüther
and
Jonas D. A. Hock

cover art by
Denis Schröder
and
Julia Klein

interior illustrations by
Bettina Burger
and
Jonathan Rudawski

special thanks to
Peter Bews

Herstellung und Verlag:
Books on Demand GmbH, Norderstedt
ISBN: 9783844813753

Font 'Foglihten' © 2011, gluk (www.glukfonts.pl gluks-za@wp.pl)
Font 'Big Top' © 2011, Shamrock (www.shamrocking.-com)

Table of Contents

Christian Schneider

The 24-Hour Man

A battered pickup truck comes stumbling from the hazy light of dawn. It rolls down the hill, down the newly paved road, and stops at the crossroads where a path leads to one of the corn farms surrounding the town. A man gets out of the truck. He yawns, scratches his unshaven cheeks and slowly stretches his sore neck.

The man isn't young anymore, he isn't old yet. Under a faded homburg dangles a hand-rolled cigarette, as he walks a few steps down the road. Then he returns to the truck and gets a hammer, some nails and a bright yellow sign, formed like an arrow, from the back of the truck, where a black man in overalls has sat up, vigorously rubbing the sleep from his eyes. The smoking man goes to a telegraph pole next to the road and nails the arrow to it, pointing out the way to the farm. He nods, maybe proudly, but still like someone who knows what's yet to come. He gets back into the truck and drives down the track.

A slap wakes the freckled boy dozing on the shotgun seat, while the black man has already started assembling the gear from the truck bed. The man in the homburg takes a spade and walks down to the field that will be their lot tomorrow. He takes a long look at it and sighs. It's not a particularly disappointed sigh, but still a sigh. He walks down to the edge of the field and rams the spade into the earth.

From now on, the man is very busy. The condition of the lot is tested and judged more than once. Stakes are driven into the ground, ropes are laid out. Slowly, the layout takes shape around the yet invisible King Pole. Here, enough space for the big cats' cages. There, a little bit of leeway for another trailer. The man has all the measurements written down in a small notebook in his jacket, but he never takes a look at it. Maybe it's because the jacket soon lies on the ground a few feet away from him. Big spots of sweat appear on his shirt, as the morning sun of July rises curiously over the hill, observing him and his black companion working almost silently.

At one point the farmer arrives in his car, watching skeptically as his field is turned into a giant blueprint. He has been paid, or at least should have been paid in advance, but the man in the hat still hands him the agreed deposit, which the farmer accepts with a curt grunt. He's slightly more affable when he's handed a few complimentary tickets for himself and his family. He almost manages to smile as he walks back to his Ford.

"I just want to get it back like it was. With all the tigers and elephants and him," he points at the black man, who's hammering a pole into the ground, "I hope it doesn't turn into the Congo over night." With a chopped laugh and a chopped start of the motor, he's gone.

The boy returns from town, the whole back of the truck filled with bundles of hay, half-rotten vegetables, packages of minced meat, and loads of canned goods.

"Nine goddamn grandchildren!" he shouts as he gets out of the car. "He says he wants to take them all!"

The man just nods, helping the boy and the black man unload the truck, before he takes it himself to go into town. It's what you can only call a quiet little town. The sun shines brightly on a proper main street, with barber shops, a local bank and a neat Polish restaurant. There are no chimneys spoiling the blue sky, no storehouses blocking the horizon. Nothing much has changed in the last decade and nothing much will change.

Following the straight course of Main Street, the man watches the townsfolk going about their daily business and watching him curiously in turn. He might have been here before. At least he doesn't remember, which is a good sign. He has never been beaten up here, never been spat in the face, never had to look into a shotgun barrel. Not in such a quiet little town.

The advance men have done their job scrupulously. Everywhere the clowns grin at him, the lions roar at him, the trapeze girl flirts with him. All passers-by spare them at least a short look of wonder, transfixed by the giant red letters, the impossible poses, the glamorous smiles. They didn't notice the men putting the posters up the week before. The man goes to the grocer's, whose owner collects the tickets for his grandchildren with a grin. He avoids being shown photographs of all of them. Afterwards, he still has to make a visit to the police department. He has no problems getting the permit for the show.

The chief doesn't have grandchildren, but a paraplegic mother-in-law who likes to look at the aerialists. The chief tries to make small-talk, but the man still has a lot of work to do. He steps outside, the afternoon sun blinding him for a moment.

The fatigue catches him on the way to the post office. The sun overwhelms his eyes, forcing them shut, and he has to stop and find his balance. For a minute or so, he stands very still, one hand on the picket fence next to him.

"Are you alright?"

He opens his eyes again. It's a pretty house, not beautiful but pretty. White shingles and a slate roof. A young woman has stepped out into the garden. She's pretty, not beautiful but pretty. In her big blue eyes lies concern. Perhaps because of the strange sweaty man in front of her house, perhaps because he's extremely pale and his hand is still clutching her fence.

"Thanks, ma'am. No need to worry." The man straightens up and draws in some air, as if to test himself. "Appreciate your concern, though."

"Are you sure? Would you like to come in and have a glass of water? It's no bother."

The man hesitates, maybe only for a second, smiling to himself. Then he lifts his hat and bows his head.

"Much appreciated, ma'am. But I ought to be going."

The woman smiles cautiously and returns to the pretty house, with her eyes down, not turning around again. He follows her example, slowly walking away.

The whole wall of the fire department down the road is plastered with posters. They have ensnared a little boy, seven or eight, whose serious gaze wanders around them, maybe searching for some secret among their bright colors. The truck is already visible at the end of the street, but the man stops once more. He stands next to the boy, staring silently at the posters himself.

A few moments pass. Finally, the boy acknowledges the presence of the fellow gazer, turns to him and proclaims in a voice of quiet excitement "The circus is coming to town."

"I can see that."

"Tomorrow night."

"Indeed."

"I've never been to a circus. They don't come here usually."

"Are you going to see the show?"

"I don't know. My ma decides that."

"Well, I think you should go."

The boy looks at him, a questioning look in his big blue eyes.

"I've never been to a circus," he repeats. He points at the garish promises. "Do they have all these things?"

"Do they have them? The question is what don't they have?"

This seems to puzzle the boy, so the man continues.

"I'll tell you what they have. They have the funniest clown to have ever worn giant shoes. A pretty girl, commanding the fiercest and most ferocious wild animals. A real fortune teller – they say she can see everything that will happen to you. A knife thrower. A whole army of trapeze artists, courageously flying through the air. A girl walking the tightrope, no net, just her feet keeping her from falling. A magician who can make anything appear or disappear."

The boy's eyes are getting bigger and bigger. His mouth is slightly open, but he only closes it when the man has finished, licking his dried-up lips.

"Have you seen them? All those things?"

The man pauses. He looks at the posters for a short moment. Then he smiles at the boy.

"It's been a while. I'm always somewhere else."

The boy nods seriously.

"But again, you should be going."

Two tickets have appeared in the man's left hand, and the boy stares at them, his mouth a little o of surprise.

"How did you do that?"

The man keeps on smiling, holding out the tickets.

"Take your mother, will you?"

It's night now, a half moon traveling a clear black sky sprinkled with summer constellations. The man leans on the hood of the truck, rolling the latest cigarette in the moonlight. Inside and on the truck, the boy and the black man are fast asleep. The man should get some rest as well, but instead he is awake in the chilly night air and waits, listening to the katydids.

Lighting his cigarette, he walks down to the lot again, checking the layout once, twice. It's hard to see all the markers in the semi-darkness. When there's nothing left to check, he returns to the solitude of the hood. If this is like other nights, he'll have to do even more work when the trek finally arrives. He needs to talk to the lot man, who might change his layout. Only

afterwards does he get another chance for a few hours of sleep in his bunk bed in the caravan. Before sunrise, he'll get into the truck again. He'll try to find the sun somewhere east and tell the others how to get there, with his bright yellow arrows.
He's always twenty-four hours ahead.

The glimmer of the cigarette goes out. For an endless moment, the man stares at the last few lights of the town down the valley. Then he listens. A heavy engine roars in the distance. Then another one joins in. And finally the headlights of a giant caterpillar of metal appear over the hills.

The Circus is in town.

Jasmin Friedrich

Outside the velvet curtain

Brave as the liontamer
Charming as the magician
Enchanting as the trapeze artist

Entertaining as the ring master
Funny as the clown
Elegant as the tightrope walker

Outside the velvet curtains
A liar, that's just what you are

Giuseppina Agostinetto-Lesle

Circus Life

or

the Circus of Life

The city where the circus was staying for a long time was large, so that there were many spectators every day. People referred to it as "The Circus". It was known to be big, rich and to have many good acts in it's programme – it was another world in which life began in the evening with "Ladies and gentlemen, children of all ages..." If townspeople walked around the caravans during the day, they saw circus performers who were so active, so busy working and rehearsing that they regarded them as normal workers or housewives or apprentices. Still, the circus people displayed a certain degree of playfulness; whatever they did, there was always music to be heard.

Ben spent a lot of time watching his fellow artistes practising in the ring, which was the most important place for him. Now, it was ten o'clock, time for John, the horse trainer, who had the ring to himself and his six white horses from ten to twelve. And after him, it was Paul's time to practise juggling; he shared the ring with a number of children watching him and trying their hands at acts of their own. When Paul was nearly finished, he noticed Gregory with his five little dogs.

"Hi Gregory," Paul greeted him; the dog trainer had been sitting in a corner thoughtfully, looking at his dogs, which seemed to be restless today. "Not your lucky day, I guess?" "Definitely not," Gregory replied. The dogs seemed to understand what the short exchange was about and they barked as if they were laughing at them.

At this point, Laura, the beautiful trapeze artist, stepped into the ring to begin her training. As always, she caught everybody's attention. Her fellow artistes looked at her with admiration and greeted her with a friendly hello; she returned each greeting with a smile. She was conscious of her beauty and charm, and nobody could ignore her provocative sensuality and the use she made of her enthralling body.

Ben, the trapeze catcher, was her husband – a well-built man and Laura was the love of his life. In the spotlight, when they performed their difficult acts in their skin-tight costumes, they truly seemed to fly. The spectators watched them, moving their heads to and fro, anxiously waiting for the artistes' bodies in the air to return to the safety of the pedestals. The applause was always long and enthusiastic, but the attention of the spectators was focused on her; nobody ever noticed the worried look on Ben's face.

Not long before, during a performance, Boo, the clown, had made the people laugh with his jokes about a pair of trapeze artists with their heads in the clouds. Ben felt a strange suspicion. He tried to find out more about what Boo might have had in mind, but when he talked to him he was so awkward that Boo could only make fun of his words. Eventually, Ben gave up, but not without something bitter growing in his soul – something quite sad.

Walking among the caravans, Ben enjoyed looking at the activities of his fellow performers. He knew almost all of them but, being more reserved than his wife, he passed them by with nothing more than a gentle nod. He only stopped once to offer his help to a man with a mechanical problem. Ben had a special knack for such things. When the weather was fine like today, the doors and windows of all the caravans were wide open – all activities could take place outside. He was therefore all the more surprised when he noticed that one caravan door was closed. He tried to remember to whom it belonged. The owner was a handsome new fellow artist, a knife thrower. Somebody was laughing inside; Ben hesitated, but soon went on.

In the late afternoon, most performers would be preparing themselves for the show. A lot of them, old and young, were waiting near the back entrance to the ring while the spectators slowly filled the rows of seats under the big top. Some of the artistes led animals, some had equipment for their acts. Most were quiet, others a little excited. None of them was laughing – too much depended on their discipline. Soon, one act followed another, with clowns appearing to the children's great joy in-between.

This evening, the bull handler made the elephants do something new. Even the elephants seemed to giggle as they threw small, brightly coloured balls for the audience to catch. Their last act was to walk around the ring climbing up and down the heavy bull tubs, waving their trunks.

After them Laura and Ben made their appearance. When they entered, the ring was flooded with new lights. They presented themselves in a brightness which separated them from the spectators, who remained in the dark. Everyone was aware of their ability and courage; a courage which sometimes seemed imprudent. They climbed the rope ladders to reach the pedestals, the points from which they began their acrobatics. Laura was splendid; she was a marvellous flyer, swinging from one trapeze to the other, again and again, with infinite elegance. Ben caught her, sure and calm. He pressed her hands more than it was necessary to communicate his love and his need for her love.

Still, he worried more and more. Many of the things that had been on his mind began to fall into place. Often on a walk, he felt drawn to the knife-thrower's caravan. Once he could distinctly hear Laura laughing and could imagine the rest. If he happened to see her leaving her lover's caravan...but was he really her lover?

He knew that she would never leave him. He knew that she would say to every other man "Take it or leave it!" explaining perhaps that Ben was the only important man for her.

Life went on, and Ben's suffering continued. Meanwhile the Grand Gala was approaching. All the circus people felt committed to turning it into a success. The chosen day for the spectacle was a Saturday, but even on Friday many of the performers were worried; the weather was too warm and sultry. "Surely," they thought, "there's a storm coming up." In fact, towards dusk on Saturday, dark clouds filled the sky and at the beginning of the performance loud, rumbling thunder could be heard.

The show went on all the same. When Ben and Laura entered the ring together, they were greeted by enthusiastic applause. The thunder became louder; Laura and Ben were getting tense. She was returning to him with a brilliant smile on her face when the lights went out and a peal of thunder roared through the darkness. Many people cried, more in surprise than in fear. Only Laura cried in pain; she had fallen very badly into the safety net.

Circus people with lamps ran from every corner telling everybody to sit down and keep calm, while Laura was taken out of the ring with great care. The audience calmed down. The worst of the storm was over, the lights came on again.

It was a long time before Laura could take part in the circus life again, sitting at the entrance, selling tickets with her usual kindness – still beloved by everyone. Ben had given up his performances; his skill as a mechanic had become widely appreciated. Above all he had to take care of Laura, his Laura.

Sometimes, while calmly working, Ben would try to remember precisely the moment when Laura fell. He could never be sure whether the sudden darkness alone was responsible for his failure to catch her.

Jana Ulbrich

For There She Was

The ringmaster stepped heavily into the middle of the ring, leaving puffs of whirling sawdust in the air. "Time for something dangerous now," he announced in his dark voice, bowing to the audience with flashing teeth. "Time for the lion tamer!" The babbling and twaddling went quiet, becoming more of a buzzing, expectant whisper; then it died down completely. People started shuffling their feet. Someone cleared their throat. The spotlight seemed to be waiting patiently.

One by one, eight big cats gracefully set paw into the ring, filling the tent with an atmosphere of awe and horror. They were followed by the small incarnation of beauty. I had to squint and thought of rubbing my eyes, but how pointless that would be, for there she was. The girl I had lost my heart to; a woman now, with a steady walk and not the slightest hint of uncertainty about her. The little flutter of her eye-lids was gone and I felt like bursting into tears for the loss of it. But the way she stroked her hair back with was still the same. I knew it was her. I couldn't believe it. The leather whip in her hand touched the side of the panther, just slightly, but the cat reacted at once, moving to stand on its hind legs.

How old had we been? Someone had taken me with them to this huge party. I got lost right at the beginning of that evening. All of my friends had vanished, and I was more than a little drunk already. Dreamily, I felt myself drawn to the source of music like a moth to the light, and so I went, making my way through the crowd until I stood right in front of the band. I stared at them for a while, trying to arrange my thoughts. Someone yelled into my ear. Someone rudely bumped into me. Someone rolled herself a cigarette. She was standing next to me and I threw a shy glance at her; long, blonde hair, dark clothes, and she looked up from her half-finished cigarette, keeping hold of my glance.

I couldn't move. I couldn't look away. I felt hypnotized. She saw me, but it wasn't just seeing; it felt as if she was throwing light into every inner corner of myself and she knew. She knew.

Then, she released me with a little smile and continued rolling her cigarette. I turned my head away from her and stared at the band's guitar player, without hearing anything. I thought of nothing, couldn't think of anything else but her existence right next to me. When I felt her turning towards me again, I held my breath. She lit her cigarette. Our glances met again, not as deeply as before but enough to make me shiver. She inhaled, fixating me. She blew out the smoke. She smiled, again.

Then we kissed.

And I lost myself between her lips. I lost myself in the sweetness, the softness of her tongue; her intensity. When I opened my eyes again I had no more heart, and the world around us was blurred and noisy. She slowly traced my lips with her finger, and her eyes, those deep, dark eyes sucked me in.

"Tell me," I said with a voice I couldn't believe was mine - it was more of a distant, hoarse whisper - "Tell me your name."

She pretended not to hear me. She kissed me, more roughly than before and less sweet, and I tasted teeth and pushed her away, holding her at arm's length.

"No, really. I want to know. What's your name?"

Her eyelids fluttered a little, then she detached her eyes from my face. I looked at her, felt her drifting away from me, and I cautiously touched her lips the way she had touched mine before.

"Did you see that tiger, mummy?" a little girl squeaked, her braids jumping up and down as she did, in excitement. "Didn't it look like he was going to swallow her at any moment?" People got up, leaving their places to buy sweets or take their children to the ponies. I still felt a little dizzy.

You never told me your name and I never saw you again. Until now. It took me years to get over you, people were laughing about me. "Look," they said, "How can anyone you barely spoke to steal your heart?" And I couldn't explain it to them. I couldn't explain it to myself, either; and as the months passed by, this one night became more and more like a dream, a distant hallucination. Like a hole in reality, as reality is numb and colourless but you were so full of life, so vivid. So true.

And I thought, maybe you didn't want me to lose this illusion of you being special, being more, being everything I needed. Maybe you felt all empty inside, and you didn't think this was what I was looking for. But I know that we could have made it. I knew it back then.

You could have filled me up with your emptiness and I would have filled you up with mine.

Anna Kuropatkova

Welcome to the Circus

Do you remember how we went
To rainbows of the circus tent?
I was a girl with tiny plaits;
You were a skinny boy of eight.
The circus was for us that night
A swirl of colours and of light:
That funny, kind and lovely clown
Made laughter even when he frowned.
We used to dream... You used to dream
That you'd become that tall and lean...
That dressage artist on the horse
Which was adorned with flimsy gauze,
Which always galloped on and on,
Agile, magnificent and strong.

The years elapsing since those nights
Were swirls of colors and of light.
Life was a juggler from the start:
It juggled us so far apart.
Life has for those who do the flips
Potential for broken hips.
You're certainly that acrobat
Who broke his legs upon the mat.
I'm galloping without repose –
Mad mare, meager and morose.
Tell me how many times I fell?
My rider cannot ride me well.
The noise and colors, blinding light...
At least we always tried to fight,
But we found out throughout the years
That clowns always laugh through tears.

Elke J. Zenker

No Real Soothsayer

Madame Raven put her knitting down and huddled into her armchair again, drawing her skirts tight. She had been sitting here for two hours, and the cold creeping up from the ground had finally managed to get through her socks and the blanket she had placed across her lap. She was wearing every skirt she possessed, but still freezing and stiffening up in the autumn breeze. It was no use to keep knitting when she could barely bend her fingers, and so she placed her knitting under her chair and got her muff. She preferred to simply sit in her armchair and look out to the field in front of the circus which she could see through the open entrance of her little tent.

The show wouldn't be beginning any time soon, although the sun was about to set. There were no clients yet. There had hardly been any clients of late. The circus had overstayed its welcome and would soon be packing up and travelling to its winter quarters further south, where it was warmer; and not as dark and cold as here. Madame Raven sighed and shifted to find a more comfortable position. She might just as well make some tea, even though Jack wouldn't be coming anymore...

"Excuse me, are you open?" Madame Raven opened her eyes, startled. Had she fallen asleep again? When had it grown so dark? "I'm sorry, I woke you up." A young girl was standing in the entrance, blocking the light of the circus lanterns from outside.
"No, no, I was simply taking a closer look at the inside of my eyes. Come in, dear, and close the curtain, will you?"
   From inside her muff Madame Raven drew a box of matches and lit the petroleum lamp, which she kept to the side of her armchair on a little table. The warm glow that instantly filled the little tent also helped to hide the wear and tear of Madame Raven's belongings. Even though it was still cold in the tent, at least it looked warm and cosy.
"I don't need a reading. The woman in the ticket booth told me to come here."
The girl was still standing in the entrance as if she didn't know what to do.
 "I'm looking for Jack."
Madame Raven sighed and closed her eyes. Who wasn't looking for Jack? As if she

knew where he was, just because he was her son. Madame Raven tried to take another look at the girl, but her eyes weren't as good as they used to be. However, she could still see that the girl wasn't even thirteen, yet. Was she alone? Something felt wrong. The girl looked tense. Or was it something in her voice? It didn't matter; a long life as a fortune-teller had taught Madame Raven to trust her feelings.

"Why don't you sit down for a minute, dear? I don't have any clients anyway and you look like you could do with a rest and some hot tea."

Madame Raven was glad; she'd have company with her tea after all and that her preparations hadn't been in vain. She didn't wait for a reply and lit the little gas stove, so the smell of gas spread inside the tent and mingled with that of the petroleum.

"I don't have time. I need to see Jack. Is he with the animals?" The girl had turned around again, which made it a lot harder to read her. "He's not with the animals," Madame Raven hurried to say before the girl was off. "He ran away."

Maybe if she had looked at the girl more closely, she could have predicted the girl's reaction and would have been a bit gentler, but despite her profession, she had no supernatural gift whatsoever and simply relied on common sense and her feelings. That meant, she made mistakes; her life was proof of that. When the girl broke out in tears she was not prepared and stared at her for a second before she walked around the table. When she put her arms around the girl to comfort her, Madame Raven knew the problem. Oh my God, she was still a little girl herself! How could this have happened?

"Oh you poor thing! Don't cry. It'll be okay. We'll get this mess sorted out, don't worry."

It had been years since Madame Raven had rocked anybody for comfort, and was surprised to notice how nice it felt to hold someone in her arms again, even if it was a total stranger. She loved her boy, of course, but he'd been real trouble in the last few years. The girl was still crying and as usual, Madame Raven could barely manage to prevent herself from crying, too. Maybe it was her profession or her big heart, but other people's misery often upset her. She wished she could hold her for a while longer to allow herself and the girl to calm down, but it wasn't good for the baby or the mother-to-be to sit on the ground in autumn. She forced the girl up and into the other armchair, which was facing her own. Madame Raven sat down across the table, but held on to the girl's hand, gently stroking it. The crystal ball she always kept in the middle of the table to meet her client's expectations was in the way and she was about to put it away, when the girl stopped her.

"Leave it, please. Can you not help me find Jack with it? Or read my future?"
Her despair and hope went straight to Madame Raven's heart. She had always used the crystal ball as a magnifying glass. During a reading she could stare at it as long as she wanted and study her client to figure out what they wanted or needed to hear. There was nothing supernatural

about it or about Madame Raven. She couldn't read the future.

There used to be a another Madame Raven with the circus who had a gift with the crystal ball and the cards and when she had not been Madame Raven yet, but had still been called Laura and had asked for an apprenticeship, the late Madame Raven had told her that it was nothing you could learn. You either had the gift or you didn't – and Laura didn't. Somehow she had persuaded Madame Raven and 'learnt' the trade anyway; honed her knowledge of human nature and discovered how to read people. She had always loved her profession, loved to help people. But she knew her limits and what she was: a well-meaning con artist.

What a mess her life was. The old Madame Raven had warned her that it would end badly and that this was not her fate, but Laura had insisted, begged, pleaded... and now her body had betrayed her twice. First when she was born without a gift, and a second time when it had the audacity to bear a boy. Not a girl, to whom she could teach her trade, to ensure that a Madame Raven would continue to exist. Oh Lord, what a mess... such a mess and on top of that a pregnant child, who had probably run away from home. Had Jack known? Was that why he'd left? If she sent the girl home, would he come back to her?

"I'm sorry, dear. But I can't." She was about to put the ball away, when the girl grabbed at it and ... froze; her hand on top of the glass. For a moment she was still, then the girl sighed, sat back in her chair and smiled at Madame Raven for the first time. "No, he won't be back," the girl said. There were still tear stains on her cheeks, but she looked relaxed and comfortable. "I'm sorry, Laura, that I burst into your life like this." Madame Raven didn't know what to say. She had never seen anybody's attitude change so fast. The desperate little girl who had walked in moments ago was gone and was now a confident, young mother-to-be.

In the back of the tent, the kettle started to whistle and the girl got up to make some tea. Laura watched her from the chair. For a moment she wondered whether she should help, but the girl seemed to know where everything was. Laura looked around in the tent at all the familiar things and loved pieces. All this here belonged to Madame Raven; but, as the girl had said, her name was Laura. She had expected to be resentful or something similar; instead she was relieved, as if she had shed a skin that had grown too tight.

"If you don't mind, I'd like to stay," the girl said.

Denis Schröder

Aymara

When she woke up, Aymara could still feel the wet grass tickling between her toes, the hot, humid air filling her nostrils and the taste of papaya penetrating the buds of her tongue. She remembered the smell of the trees that filled the village's centre square surrounded by little wooden huts, where she used to play with the other children. She remembered her mother looking out to her through the small hole that was the kitchen window, busily preparing lunch, cutting the yuca roots with the large kitchen knife to pour into the stew. And she remembered the whiteness of her teeth and the softness of her voice when she called her name. They used to call her João back then. Back then, everything had been much simpler.

Diffuse grey morning light fell through the small windows of her caravan and painted dark shadows under Aymara's eyes and around her chin and cheekbones. Outside, the entire troupe was already up and a-rumbling. The young men were putting up the tents and stalls, shouting sharp and angry commands through the dry air. A faint cry of an elephant from within one of the cages on the opposite side of the compound reached her ear. After a bumpy ride through the vast nothingness of the prairie, the circus had arrived in yet another indistinguishable, sand-coloured town that would facilitate shelter and provisions in exchange for some diversion and entertainment before the troupe would have to pack up again and move on to their next destination. Tired, and with sore limbs, Aymara sat in front of the large, ornately decorated mirror and occupied herself with her morning toilette.

She rarely ever dreamed of her childhood these days. Throughout her life she had avoided looking back into the past. She dreaded the horrid and deformed reflection of herself that would stare back at her from the looking glass. At the age of fourteen or fifteen her body started to cast off the shape of a child and she abandoned the village that she had grown up in, and left to try her luck in the city. São Paulo, at the time, seemed the most likely place to offer a life worth living. The century was hardly a decade old and the city was brimming with people from all over the world trying to make a fortune in the rapidly growing metropolis. It was here that she put on lipstick and painted her eyelashes for the first time. Make-up bought with the money from one of her first customers, an Italian entrepreneur, who had picked her up in one of the forlorn, derelict streets on the outskirts of the city. And it was here that she adopted her new name. At first, Aymara felt hesitant and ashamed to expose her distorted self to paying strangers, but soon discovered that feeling disconnected to one's own body was only helpful when one wanted to exploit it. Back then, she would not have been able to even find herself in those labyrinthine alleys, tarted up with flickering red lights and tawdry music, but the customers always did. Many of them were businessmen, some of them artists, and despite their flamboyancy and cosmopolitanism, most of them had a wife and children waiting for them at home. For the men who requested her services, she was just one of the many curiosities the city had to offer. When they were with her, they would tell her about eunuchs in gold saris dancing in the temples of Bombay, pay her to seduce them like a youth in the audience of a Parisian revue, and lament the decline of the castrati in

Italy and they would read to her from obscure magazines about the fantastical experiments of pioneering doctors in Berlin.

A hesitant knock on the door awoke Aymara from her daydreaming. It was Will standing outside, on the iron grid that led up to her caravan, on his break, in the heat of midday, probably with a cigarette in his hand, and sweat running down his temples and over his neck. "Aymara, are you up yet?" His insecure voice resembled that of a boy more than that of a man. Sometimes, Aymara wondered whether he was even able to grow a beard. Sometimes, she hated him.

"Cretino!" She cried, looking over her left shoulder as if addressing him without the walls of the caravan between them. "I told you never to disturb me so early in the morning."

She hadn't dared to talk to him ever since their last encounter. She was afraid of the way he would look at her now, in the revealing light of day. Now that he had seen.

"It's just, last night was pretty rough. I wanted to see if you're okay. And also, the ringmaster said he wanted a word with you."

"Tell him I'll meet him once I'm done here." Her fingers trembled as she forced her earrings through the holes in her lobes. After a brief pause she heard his aggrieved footsteps retreating from her caravan, realizing that he couldn't hope for another word from her for the moment. She looked at herself in the mirror with disgust.

São Paulo needed only a few years to wear her out. She felt crowded, and sometimes, she was overcome by the urge to break out of her own body. She began to feel an aversion to the way people treated and looked at her. Here, she would never be the woman she so longed to be and a feeling of restlessness started to grow in her chest again. She would never again stay in one place long enough for it to leave behind any footprints on the battered tapestry of her memory. When she arrived at the circus, she tried to seclude herself as much as possible from everyone around her. It was the prerogative of the tightrope walker to live and work by herself, without interference from any of the other showmen in the troupe. Aloof, in the stifling air of the big top, which sometimes felt too thick to inhale, she was pervaded by a thrilling feeling of numbness and seclusion. The fancy costumes, made of sequins and pearls, and the large feathers in her hair she would wear for herself rather than the audience admiring her from the ground as she balanced elegantly above their heads. Will had been with the circus his entire life; and while he lacked any particular talent that would have qualified him for a spot in the ring, he made an excellent animal keeper due to his kind nature and generous heart. She had noticed his sheepish glances from the sidelines as she performed, and was drawn to the simplicity and truthfulness in his expression, qualities she thought were absent in herself. He was too simple-minded to see her as anything other than the woman that she was. Even when she told him, he was calm and understanding. Then she undressed herself in front of him for the first time, to make love to him. Her back was turned towards him, but he knowingly pressed his body tight against hers. She felt his breath in her hair and realized that he was smiling as he tenderly kissed the back of her head. He was the only one who knew.

The dusty ground felt like emery paper under Aymara's soles as she walked towards the caravan of the ringmaster. When the door opened, a cloud of cheap men's perfume and tobacco smoke escaped from inside and wrapped itself around her face. Upon entering, she became aware of the presence of someone sitting opposite the ringmaster's desk. It was a tall elderly man in a black suit and a top hat, indecently sucking on a cigar. She had seen him before, but couldn't quite remember when, and under what circumstances. They greeted her and bade her sit down on the one free chair in the room.

"Aymara, this here is an old friend of mine," commenced the ringmaster in a solemn tone gesturing towards the stranger sitting next to her. "And he told me that the two of you are acquainted as well, and that he was thrilled to discover you're staying here with our circus."

She felt a sudden terror flickering through the muscles under the skin of her face.

"I hardly believe that a lady as beautiful as our dear Aymara would remember an old man like myself," smiled the gentleman and put out his cigar in the ashtray in front of him.

"We met while I was staying in Brazil a few years back."

"He says he has an exciting offer to make."

Down below, the audience held their breath as Aymara set her foot on the wire. The brightly coloured dress wrapped tightly around her torso glistened in the spotlights, which were directed towards nothing but her. Long rounds of applause and suspenseful gasps filled the tent as she acrobatically bent herself over the tight-rope. Beads of sweat ran down her face and occasionally dripped down to the sawdust that covered the floor of the ring. Her step felt unsteady. To her right, the stranger sat self-assuredly among the audience and clapped along whenever Aymara had performed another stunt. His offer was still resounding in her head. Once again she felt imprisoned and a need to jump out of her own skin. Even if she refused to go with him, she could not stay with the circus. She was so vulnerable and exposed. No matter how high up she went with the tightrope, the spotlight would follow her. The curtain of isolation she had always been hiding behind was falling down, unveiling the faces that were curiously staring in her direction from the other side. In the corner of her eye, on the opposite side of the ring, she saw Will, her dear Will, standing in one of the deserted entrances, looking up to her with a glum expression on his face. And as she danced across the wire, her heart grew heavy in her chest, and she realized that she no longer had the strength in her arms to hold up the balancing pole to keep her from falling.

Tina F. Hüther

White Linen

When I was a young girl I started to object to my life. When I read through the one book my father had ever given me "Pippi Longstocking" I always wanted to be more like Annika. I refused to think of myself as Pippi. In reality I was a copy of the protagonist of the book and had little in common with a pretty, clean girl in a velvet dress. My father is the ringmaster and head clown of a circus. Since my mother died when I was very young, another hated similarity with Pippi Longstocking, I never had matching socks; I was always searching for my hand-kerchiefs, and this search was carried out over a huge terrain of carriages and boxes that was inhabited by clowns who had the unnerving character trait of never giving a concrete answer. This is how I grew up. I saw the girls in their white ruffled dresses who came to the circus to have fun and my hatred grew as they paraded by me, smiling little innocent smiles and talking about how "exciting" and "wonderful" the circus was. The circus seemed to have that appeal to all the visitors. All the perversion of ugly men, trick magic, women with drug problems, too bright lights and overpriced popcorn seemed to make visitors happy. When I turned 16, my father said that I should pick a job in the circus. I thought long and hard about the opportunities. Finally I decided to work at the box office. Every night I sat there and made little stacks of tickets: The red ones for the adults, the white ones for the children. I sorted them into little stacks and switched them around. I thought hours about perfecting the process and every minute was pure delight. I perfected the position of my hand for when I gave the visitors their tickets. Later I tried matching nail polish, first to the colour of my skin then to the colours of the tickets. When I got older I matched my outfit to the box I was sitting in. When I turned 18 I started to wear white blouses every day. By that time, I had been working in the box office for two years and I had loved every minute of it. Every day, I looked forward to the evening. During the day I stayed in my little part of the caravan I shared with my father and practised my body language. It was important to me to avoid the madness and chaos outside. I took great delight in reading old account books, thought about

organizing patterns and dreamed about white folders and linen. Outside, the freaks, lions and "magicians" were talking, playing and shouting while I was doing my embroidery. My father insisted on talking to me quite often, but most of the time he was drunk and smelly. I didn't like to talk to him because he was always making rude jokes, and when he was drunk he talked about dancers, as if they were a) a good thing and b) something a decent person would like to be.

Then, two months ago, it happened. I was sitting in the box office, dreaming about new folders, when I saw him for the first time. He was wearing a grey suit and was of average height. His brown, short hair and bushy eyebrows, as well as the suitcase he had with him, made him look older.

44

Upon giving him his ticket, little finger stiff in the air, I asked him:"Sir, why do you have this suitcase with you?" The answer came as prompt and proper as one could wish, "because I work in a bank". He then nodded, smiled at me and entered the tent.

When I went to the post office the next day I saw him again. As I smiled shyly while performing the delightful task of sorting mail we got to talking over an address, while I was staring in embarrassment at the false stamps which the circus people had put on the envelopes. Encouraged by his dis-regard of the mess, I told him about the chaos in my life, of the screaming freaks and of my drunk father.

We left town the next day and continued touring through Virginia, Oklahoma and North Carolina. I bought some fancy looking stationery and wrote to him every Thursday. I told him a lot about my life and he told me interesting things about his. About his work placement at the bank, where he worked as an accountant and about his love for stamps. At first, I thought that I was only a fancy of his – writing to a circus girl who has an "exciting" life and was "on the road". But after some months, he agreed that my circumstances were unbearable, and he confessed his interest in me.

The next night I ran away.

Now I'm sitting in our house. When I look over the fence, I see my lovely neighbours, Mr. and Mrs. Rochester, leaving their home. The green of the lawn rivals the white of the tablecloth, which I caress and smooth out with the tips of my fingers. While I put cream-coloured porcelain dishes onto the table, with perfectly manicured fingers, I smile at the simple beauty of the action itself within the calm activity of preparing our dinner. I wait for my husband to arrive. I marvel at the white fence in front of our house. Finally, I feel calm, happy and at home.

Julia Klein

Tame

When Alan saw her for the first time, he thought she was the last person in the world he expected to tame wild animals. Danielle was small, slender and graceful as a young deer. She had smooth, pale skin and shining waves of golden hair. Her defined features and beautiful neck could have been the work of a painter. With amber eyes and a voice like honey, she put a smile on everybody's faces. No one knew her age, but the old man who worked at the box office swore that she had been in the company as long as he could remember. Yet Danielle couldn't be beyond thirty.

It was obvious to most people that her personality had to be as flawless as her angelic looks suggested. But Alan knew it was not. He had been raised in the South, a good Christian, and couldn't help but consider her conduct indecent. Sure, the turn of the century was close, and Alan had noticed that people were changing. Nowadays, it was expected of a circus artist to be indecent in one way or another

(it added to the atmosphere, they said).
When he had been a child, richer folks
were rarely seen in the circus; today, they
came for the spectacle as well as for the
impropriety. Danielle, however, treated
this as a matter of course, and saw no
reason to pretend otherwise. She took
lovers without as much as a bashful glance.
She never uttered a nervous laugh when
someone spotted her behind her caravan;
only the slightly reddened cheeks as she
emerged from it in the morning bore
witness to things Alan tried hard not to
think of. Danielle was often in his dreams.
But when he woke, he felt ashamed -
maybe because, as far as he could tell, she
never did.

Not long ago, on a mild spring night, he had
a chance to observe her latest conquest.
Alan was passing by her caravan on his
way to meet a couple of friends, when he
heard her door creak open. For some
reason, the hair on the back of his neck
tingled. "Alan?" He turned around to see
her standing in the doorway, surrounded
by a blurry glow of light. His heart beat a
little faster. Danielle was still in her show
outfit, but bare-footed and dishevelled. Her
blouse was unbuttoned half-way, her hair
hung down in messy strands.

"I heard you walking by, you got a minute?"

"Sure," he heard himself say. He wondered how she had known he was there.

"You're a darling. See I have a guest over and we are of a mind to celebrate."

A cloud of warm, perfumed air swept out of the caravan. Alan could hear another person moving inside. "Your friend John told me that he was in possession of a genuine French brandy that he had absolutely no use for," she said. That was a lie, of course. Johnsie made generous use of his not-so-secret stash of alcohol. The brawny man always offered Alan a drink, but he'd accepted it only once. Afterward he had felt sick. It was offensive to consider Danielle even holding one of those grimy bottles. But she continued, "Since I have nothing to offer to my guest, this would really save me from embarrassment. Could you go and ask him for it?"

Alan took off his cap and raked his hair.

"A-are you sure? I wouldn't vouch for the, er, quality of John's, er, imports. Beggin' your pardon."

"Oh it'll be all right. Just go and get it for me, will you?"

"Of course, yes," he mumbled,

"I was on my way there, anyway." He fumbled with his cap and quickly walked off.

49

Alan's mind raced. This was new. He usually just cleaned the cages in the morning, while she was training her animals outside. He brought them their food every night, and made sure every cage was safely locked at all times. This was the first time Danielle had talked to him about anything substantial beyond his job. She had not just commented on the show or the weather. He felt almost elated, but immediately checked himself. There was a man in her caravan, probably the tall, slender stranger he had seen her with the day before. The thought of what they were doing seemed so wrong that Alan clenched his fist in anger. Danielle was so pure and gentle, he just couldn't bear the thought of... it was too much. He wanted to swoop in, save her from this dingy circus caravan, build her a house, and...

"Twos! Billy, you dirty mongrel!" Alan heard the sound of coins on a wooden table, the clink of bottles and raucous laughter. His companions had gathered in the small, patched helper's tent next to Billy Bluebell's caravan. When Alan entered, Billy was collecting his few coins' worth of winnings. Terry stubbed his cigarette out in an ashtray and nodded to him in greeting. The quiet man lent a helping hand to pretty much everyone around the circus, and was as close to being Alan's friend as any of them got. Johnsie dealt the next round.

"Alan! Pull up a chair, laddie," he barked. "Whiskey?"

Alan pulled off his cap again and wiped his forehead. The air was sticky.

"Actually, Danielle sent me," he began, and the others stared. They all admired her and envied him his job.

"She mentioned that you promised her some of your ...stuff?"

"Yes! Yes, for sure I did!" Johnsie got up too quickly and knocked over his chair. He disregarded it and ushered Alan out of the tent. On the way to his caravan, he made

Alan repeat the entire dialogue between him and Danielle.

"Did she say anything else? About me?"

"No," Alan said, "but I don't see why you promised her that vile stuff anyway."

"Well, she wants it now, don't she?" John coughed self-importantly. Alan had nothing to counter that. If that was what she wanted, she would get it. Yet, he felt that there was much more to her than that, and she proved it every night in the arena.

Alan always watched from the side-entrance, after he had opened the small cage-door to let the cats into the arena. Every time, he heard the soft sigh that went through the audience on Danielle's appearance. The cats followed her into the brightly lit ring, and waited for her command. Then, Danielle began her dance. Horribly romantic as that sounded, Alan couldn't think of a better word for it. Was everything she did a dance? Even when she opened filthy bottles of liquor for strangers? John woke Alan from his reverie when he noisily rummaged through his collection of bottles. Finally, he pulled out a relatively clean one filled with an amber liquid.

"Here. Give your lady my compliments, eh? And no swigs!" Alan assured him that he had no interest in that, and left. As soon as Alan approached Danielle's caravan, she opened the door. She was even more flushed than before, and her hair tumbled over her shoulder. Alan handed her the bottle, too embarrassed to speak. She thanked him quickly, winked and disappeared. He heard a man's voice from inside and her soft laughter. Alan felt his cheeks burn and quickly walked away.

He couldn't sleep that night. He tried in vain to get her face out of his mind, tried to forget the smell of her caravan and her laughter. The next morning, he was still stifling yawns when he went to fetch water for the cats. When he got back, she was standing by the cages. And she wasn't alone: She had come to show the animals to her lover - the tall, handsome fellow as Alan had suspected. He had thick, light blonde hair, and a square, clean-shaven chin. Alan was shocked that the man was no older than himself. He blushed. Danielle wished him a good morning, as he proceeded to do his chores. Danielle owned seven large cats - they were hers, not the circus's and should she leave, the company would lose one of its most prized attractions: three large Bengal tigers, one black panther, two leopards, and, the only female, a lioness. They were lodged in simple iron cages that stood in a semi-circle, to allow visitors to view the animals outside the shows. Alan was fond of the cats, and they knew him well – that was how he explained their placid behaviour towards him. As he began shoveling out dirty straw, he strained his ears to overhear what Danielle and her guest were talking about.

"I acquired these," she pointed to the leopards, "when I was with another company. We toured Europe," she added. "Oh and look at her, isn't she a beauty?"

The man didn't really pay attention. He ignored Danielle's rapt explanations and tried to grasp her arm instead. But she kept moving along the cages, eluding his touch. What an idiot he was – if someone were to capture Danielle's true affections, it would be through her animals. The couple reached the tiger cage, where he was working. Finally, the man succeeded, and wormed his arm around her waist. She turned to him, smiling, when a sudden growl erupted from the tiger right next to Alan. All three cats jumped up and focused on their mistress, slowly moving towards the bars. Alan gripped the shovel tighter. The door was right behind him, but could he undo the latch before they were on him?

The man chuckled.

"Look, my sweet, they're jealous."

Danielle didn't smile. She stepped out of his embrace, towards the bars. The tigers retreated and settled down, staring. Danielle exchanged a quick glance with Alan, grabbed her guest and left. He stood frozen on the spot. Until that moment, the animals had never made the slightest move towards him. When he had started working in the circus, Danielle had explained that he needn't be afraid, because her animals were so well-trained. Alan had believed her, for some reason, and had, time and again stepped into the cage, trying to look manly and fearless. He had never been harmed, the cats had not even shown the slightest interest in him. Were they really jealous? He felt his anger rise – was he not worthy of their jealousy? Of course not. He was just the cage-keeper. He could only dream his dreams and get back to shoveling dirt in the morning.

Although he was exhausted, Alan went to see the others again that night. On his way, he made sure to give Danielle's caravan a wide berth. The cards were dealt, and when Johnsie offered whiskey, Alan accepted. He ignored their surprised stares. The vile taste quickly burned away his reservations, yet not his irritation. At some point he told them what had happened that morning, but Johnsie simply laughed at him. Alan wanted to punch him for the humiliation. But then he remembered he didn't even know how to do that, so he drank more whiskey instead.

Much later, he stumbled back through the dark camp, trying to find his tent. There it was, just past Danielle's caravan. An eerie light was coming from her windows, as if there was a fire. He crept closer to the wagon and leaned against the wooden panels. They were warm. The small window above him was slightly ajar. He reached for it, and touched the frame. It took a few seconds for him to realize his fingers were burning. Wincing, he pulled them back. The frame was boiling hot. Then he heard them. Alan's face flushed. He wasn't supposed to be standing there, yet he couldn't leave. The sounds seemed oddly far away, as if the caravan was a large hall instead. He heard words in a language he couldn't understand. Was Danielle singing? The words became a tumble in his mind. It was just the booze, he told himself. No more whiskey from Johnsies. Slowly, the world around him dissolved, until there was only the singing, and the wood beneath his searing hands. The perfumed air made his head swim, and then darkness surrounded him.

When he awoke, he found himself staring at the canvas ceiling of his tent. Dust motes were floating in a beam of light. His mouth tasted stale as he moved his dry tongue. He blinked and tried to sort through the memories of the night before. Suddenly, dream-like images flashed across his mind, remnants from his drunken stupor: Danielle's worried face, her soft hands on his body. Intense heat. The young man, eyes like fire, mouth opened to scream. The weight of a large animal on top of him, tearing off his flesh.

Alan trembled and sat up slowly. He found a bucket with water, drank from it, washed and pulled on a shirt. (When had he taken off his shirt?) Outside, the sun was shining, it was almost mid-day. Why had no one woken him? Alan started walking towards the cages, still in a daze. Terry ran into him. "Alan! Where have you been?" He looked him over. "Too much of Johnsie's, eh?" Alan nodded. "That bastard."

Terry slapped his shoulder. "Ah well, now you know. You better sober up quickly, you've got work to do!" They heard a little commotion ahead. There was a large, new cage next to the others. A crowd had gathered around it. They saw Danielle standing there, the ringmaster, and a few of the other performers. People were whispering and spreading the news.

"A puma, out of nowhere!"

"...got here just this morning, everyone taken by surprise!"

"...ringmaster was furious, had no notice whatsoever...!"

"Oh, Alan, there you are!" Alan's heart was hammering in his chest as Danielle came over to them. The sounds of last night came rushing back to him.

"Look what we've got! Isn't he fantastic?" She didn't wait for his answer, but took him by the arm, leading him a little away from the crowd.

"There's so much to do: we'll need a bigger supply of food, more water, find a place for him in the show – but you can handle all of this, can't you, Alan? You're so good with organizing these things!" She smiled her most adoring smile.

"S-sure," he managed. "Wonderful!" And with that, she left to adore her newest possession.

Alan mechanically got to work. His thoughts rushed from the sounds and smells of the night, to the cat, to Danielle... why hadn't she told anyone a new cat was arriving? Where had she gotten the money from to buy such a rare animal in the first place? But after a short while, he had exhausted himself. Besides, it was hardly his place to worry about circus policies. He did everything Danielle had asked of him, and by late afternoon finally got back to the cages. The crowd had dispersed, for now, and this corner of the camp had become relatively quiet.

When he picked up the shovel, Alan felt a dull pain in his hands. He turned them over and noticed burning marks on his palms and fingers. A thin layer of skin already covered the injuries. That was strange. He couldn't think of any time he had hurt his hands, let alone burnt them. And why hadn't he noticed this earlier? He scratched off a little scab and frowned. Something made him look up, and he saw the puma pacing in his cage. Alan dropped the shovel and walked over to him. He grabbed the bars of the cage. For a moment, the two regarded each other; then the puma came closer. Alan held out his hand, and the animal sniffed. He shoved his head underneath Alan's hand, as he'd done with Danielle. So, not even this one is jealous, Alan thought, and absentmindedly scratched the big cat between the ears. It seemed Danielle had worked her charms again.

Double Act

"Have you seen Thomas? He's my brother." I felt a tugging on my sleeve. As I looked down, I saw the pale-faced child who must have spoken to me. He was wearing short trousers, mended with colourful patches, and a little brown cap hid most of his sandy hair. His face was delicate but painted in a shocking white with crimson lips. It shocked me, somehow, to see a child like this. It would have been impossible back in Britain, I was sure... But the boy seemed so earnest that I almost thought it must be a matter of life and death for the little urchin and chose to overlook his countenance. "No, I'm sorry, I haven't," He looked so utterly disappointed that I felt compelled to add "Maybe I can help you to look for him?" He shook his head and ran away, leaving me puzzled at this sudden encounter.

When I arrived at home that night, Flora and Tilly were standing in the hallway, giggling madly. I know I should have said something, scolded them, but I am much too lenient as an employer. "What is going on here?" I asked, nonetheless, and Flora, who had been kitchen maid in my household for nearly two years, curtsied politely, and had the good sense to stop laughing. "Mr Blackwood, sir, the Circus is in town!" she said, bobbing up and down with sheer excitement. "The Circus, I see..." So Tilly and Flora would probably be expecting me to give them a day off. Well, I could probably handle a day without my servants and, to be honest, it might be even relaxing for me.

My younger sister had died some months ago after a long illness. It was the New England climate, it hadn't agreed with her. She had been ill ever since we moved to the States and her health had constantly deteriorated until last winter... Her death meant that I was now in charge of the household and of the servants, and I had to admit that I didn't do very well. I had never quite known how to deal with the lower classes and had proved to be unable to direct them. Ever since I had started to manage the servants, they had started to become unmanageable, as if to prove my own incompetence. I didn't blame myself completely – it was those American girls with their new ideas and expectations... My sister, even though hardly older than Flora and Tilly themselves, would have known how to deal with the girls, but I was helpless. I merely left them with a few instructions for the morning and retreated upstairs to my own room.

I lit the gaslight and sat down at my desk to read in the new book that I had ordered from England. It was a debut novel by a young colleague of mine, a doctor, who had written about some sort of detective. It was very new and hadn't got a lot of attention from the readership in London, but a friend of mine had recommended it to me, so I was willing to give it a try. Maybe it was all that reading about the Science of Deduction, but I suddenly remembered the little boy and came to a conclusion of my own: the pale-faced child had probably been part of the Circus. Of course, that explained the unusual paint on his face and accounted for the strangeness of the child. I did not even know why the child bothered me so much but his behaviour made it very hard for me to forget the short encounter. When I went to bed, I could not help but see the small, pale face in front of me.

The next day, the whole city was bustling with news about the Circus. They were camping on the outskirts of town, where they had arrived yesterday morning. I wondered how I could have missed the whole excitement the day before, but then, I had spent most of my time in the practice, talking to my elderly patients. Today, even they could not contain themselves with all their gossiping about the Circus. Some of them had never seen a circus and were almost overwhelmed with excitement, looking forward to the performance. Others were skeptical and some were downright disgusted by what they described as 'the moral debasement which the Circus represents." Mrs Robinson went as far as to claim that some of the circus children must have stolen her spectacles - which I knew to be somehow exaggerated since they were right there, hanging from a ribbon around her neck. Even I got a little excited about the whole thing.

When I stepped out of my house, I immediately saw the boy again. He was running up to everybody on the street, feverishly asking "Have you seen Thomas?", again and again. Finally, he came to me, looking almost hopeful. "Have *you* seen Thomas?" I was about to answer when the child let out a small shriek and ran a few steps away from me. Curious, I watched as the boy started bouncing up and down, laughing happily. He seemed to have wrapped his arms around something or someone, but I couldn't see anyone near the child. I went over to him but even before I could ask, the child looked up to me, beaming with joy. "I've found him!" he told me, and I looked at him in wonder. "Who? Who have you found?" The boy looked at me, as if I was missing the obvious. "My brother, of course," he stated, quite matter-of-factly, before hopping away, apparently holding someone by the hand. I shook my head, astonished.

Over the next couple of days, I kept seeing the boy, vividly engaged in conversation with his invisible playmate. I began to think that he had never had a sibling in the first place, and had invented someone to play with. It was simple enough, really, but it had a disturbing note to it that I couldn't quite grasp. The child seemed so happily involved in his made-up conversations that it should have been charming but... no. There was something about all this that made me uneasy. Nobody else seemed to have noticed, and I was half thinking that I was imagining things – even doctors are sometimes susceptible to passing fancies. I even went so far as to purposely avoid the child, because, frankly, the child's behaviour had an eerie quality to it. But, of course, it wouldn't do.

The Circus hadn't been here for long before I was asked to examine one of the animal carers, who had hurt his hand while helping to set up the tent. It just so happened that the child was playing not very far from us, singing 'ring-a-ring-a-roses' and dancing in a circle with someone who wasn't there. "He is an odd child..." I ventured to say, and Alan, my patient, looked up, confused. "Who?" I nodded towards him, and Alan followed my gaze. "Oh..." he said quietly, "that's Rosie...the poor child..." I looked again. "A girl? But... why is she dressed like this?" Alan sighed. He seemed to be genuinely worried for her. "...it's because of her brother, you know..." I stared at him. "Her brother? Not... not her twin Thomas by any chance?" Alan nodded. "Well yes, Thomas, exactly... He died about two weeks ago..." Alan seemed deeply concerned – the poor child... "God save his soul... Ever since then she has dressed like him..." the circus man added solemnly, and I nodded slightly. This new revelation made me shiver. I knew Rosie was just pretending at talking to her brother.

Because she wished her sibling was still there, and I knew how that felt... But still, her one-sided conversations were even more uncanny, now that I knew what reason lay behind them...

I didn't know what to say – thankfully, Alan considered his consultation over, anyway, nodded a greeting, and went away to clean the animal cages. I was left alone with Rosie and her quiet, creepy singing. My first instinct was to go and leave the little girl behind but I couldn't quite bring myself to do it. Somebody had to take care of this girl. She needed to be looked after and I had to make sure that somebody did. I could not have explained why it suddenly seemed so important to me to make sure that she was properly cared for, but so it was... With this in mind, I went over and knelt beside her while she kept dancing. "Rosie..." I said, quietly. She stopped, and looked at me. "Hello. I've seen you before. Have you met my brother?" I gulped. "I...er... no, Rosie... you see, I can't... he's gone..." Granted, this was not the most sensitive way of telling her, but then I was a doctor, a man of science, not of emotion... She didn't seem to take it too hard, just looked at me again, as if I was not quite getting what was going on. "I *know* that... but can't you see, he's still playing with me... I found him again." Rosie didn't mind me not replying because she was busy playing again. I stood up and went away, lost in thought.

I really felt responsible for the child's wellbeing now. Rosie was obviously grieving and needed a proper environment to help her deal with her loss. The Circus, it seemed to me, was not very suitable for that purpose, even though Alan had been sympathetic towards Rosie. Still, she should be in a proper home, not travelling around in a circus. I was determined to get to know Rosie, figure out who looked after and persuaded them to let her live a respectable life. And maybe I would even discover why Rosie acted as she did and how I could stop her. Natually, it was one way to deal with her brother's death, but still, it seemed to me that her behaviour had a special reason. Of course, she wasn't really talking to her brother – I would not believe something so impossible as that – but she wasn't just making the whole thing up, either. She truly believed it... So I set to work in order to uncover the mystery of Rosie and start preparing for her to leave the circus.

Needless to say: it wasn't so easy... all my clever inquiries led to nothing. The circus people seemed particularly reluctant to talk to me... understandable, I was an outsider and one would only expect circus people to have a tendency to keep to themselves but it didn't help me with my 'investigation'. All I could find out was that the parents had belonged to the circus, and when they died, the children had continued travelling with the circus, cared for by several kind-hearted artists. They had a nice little trapeze act, especially interesting because they were so young, which was why they were allowed to stay, but it seemed that they had been neglected. I was right in attempting to separate Rosie from the Circus. Unfortunately, Rosie was not very cooperative, and insisted that her brother did not want her to leave. The vague feeling of eeriness that had surrounded Rosie from the start became stronger and more distinct. The circus artists' behaviour wasn't reassuring, either. Some of them actually seemed to *believe* that Rosie was talking to someone when she was obviously just making up replies to questions that had never been asked. Were they just indulging the child's fantasy in the vain hope of making her feel better, or were they really so gullible as to believe in the supernatural? Did it actually help her, I wondered? Did talking to her dead brother really relieve the grief? I know it wouldn't have helped me, not without my sister answering...

After some days of fruitless investigation, I had achieved nothing but a scolding from Rosie's brother because I had stepped on his foot – according to Rosie. I was about to give up when I heard Flora and Tilly sharing their views of the performance they had seen the previous evening. "Oh, and the trapeze act! So wonderful! It was sheer magic, wasn't it, Tilly?" Flora shrieked excitedly. It gave me a headache but it also gave me an idea. Why not visit a performance myself? I had not really thought about it as I was so busy with the practice but maybe it would do me good. Moreover, it might give me a clue as to how I could help Rosie. I bought a ticket for that night's performance and went to the site of the circus when my last patients for the night had gone away. It was just as I had expected. A loud, noisy place that smelled of wild animals, sweat and candy. I immediately knew what attracted Flora and Tilly to the place. The scents and the colours, so unlike the washing soap smell and the dull white of their aprons that they were used to... Even I could not completely resist the temptation of the Circus, and when I sat down on the creaky little bench in the audience, I felt a slight shiver of anticipation.

A glance at the programme told me that Rosie was to be the closing act. Rosie? I looked again. "Wondrous Twins on the Trapeze" – surely that was a dated programme? They could not really let Rosie perform, not with her still thinking her brother was alive... I sat through the performances with the tension constantly rising. The magician failed to enchant me, and even the eight wild cats circling around the exotic lady couldn't impress me, while I was still waiting for the little girl. She finally appeared on the rigging, in a little white dress with the white and crimson make up and her hair pinned up elaborately, exactly the colour of my sister's hair... They must have partnered her with another artist if she was still doing her act but so far she was the only one visible. I was tense. She had left the platform, was swinging from a metal bar, high in the air. Another one was coming towards her. She could never reach it. Never. If she tried to grasp it, she would fall. With no one on the other end to take her hand... Rosie would die. But what if it was true? I suddenly felt the urge to laugh. It was absurd. It couldn't be true. But if it was, then she would fly. Impossible...

I looked at the child, my hand clutched around the crumpled programme. She stretched and prepared to let go.

Martin Morath

Mr. Hobbs

Mr. Hobbs was a magician, a real magician. Unlike illusionists he could do real magic. Apart from this characteristic he was a very normal, little man. His life wasn't special. He lived in a tiny caravan and was the magician of the circus. The plants on his window ledges were always so neatly cut that you might have thought him to be a member of a gardening club. The only difference from? Others was the brass name-plate at his door: Anthony Hobbs, certified magician, spells for mending and retrieval. Below he had noted his office hours, because Mr. Hobbs liked nothing more than living in peace and harmony with his neighbours, Cisco, the clown, and Esmiralda, the acrobat. None of them was surprised when Mr. Hobbs jumped on his broom in the evening. They would greet him, exchange a few words and all in all they were happy to live their lives in peace.

Years went by like that. Mr. Hobbs was as much a part of the circus as the smell of popcorn. Once a day he would perform his show and pull one or two elephants out of his hat. This was about all the magic he was allowed to perform, since there were strict regulations concerning his extraordinary abilities. People would frequent his office hours if they had lost their glasses or a machine was broken but before every client he had to consult the code of magic law. Often he had to send the clients back home because he was not allowed to help them. Since he could not solve every problem, he was not much different from a mechanic or a civil servant. But who was without faults?

In his leisure time Mr. Hobbs loved to perfect his floral arrangements, to listen to music on his gramophone or to read. One half of his caravan was full of books, a whole library that even had a ladder. This ladder, however, was only for ornamental purposes because Mr. Hobbs would usually sit in his armchair, wave the wand with his right hand and wait for the book to glide down to him. Then he would take a sip of tea, put down the cup and open the book with a sigh while his cup was being refilled. He could spend the whole afternoon like that.

It was a placid life, and Mr. Hobbs was happy with it. Then again he did not know any other. Until the day he met Sarah...

He was just cleaning his caravan by moving his wand like a baton to the music. However, he was not conducting musical instruments but a feather duster that jumped from plate to plate until all the china in his cupboard was gleaming again. That moment a little girl stormed through the door and brought a gust of cold air with her. This distracted Mr. Hobbs so much that he made all the china bang against the ceiling. While he was looking at the girl, broken pieces of porcelain were raining down on them. "Child, what has happened?" The girl, about six or seven years old, was wearing a white dress. A normal little girl, apart from the recognisable sadness in her eyes. Floods of tears were flowing down her face, down from her cheeks to the back of her hands before finally hitting the ground. Mr. Hobbs was afraid that the girl could hurt herself standing barefoot in the broken china, so he lifted her up and went to the armchair. When he was sitting there, with the skinny girl on his legs, he repeated his question. "Child, what happened?" He stroked her back to calm her down but she only cried harder. "Sh, sh, it's ok. It's ok. Everything will be fine." Suddenly, the girl stopped crying and looked at him. The green of her eyes was a sharp contrast to her blonde hair. "I want you to bring back my mummy and my daddy. " Tears were flowing silently down her face, wetting Mr. Hobbs' shirt. "Where are your mummy and your daddy?" She looked at him, pale. "Dead! They are dead. A lorry made them dead." For a split second pictures flashed in his head. Screeching brakes, eyes wide open, splattering glass. Then he saw the girl on his lap again. "I want to have my mummy and my daddy back. You can do magic, can't you? Make them alive!"

At this moment a string snapped in Mr. Hobbs's heart. He didn't have to look it up in the code of law; he knew that he could not do it. To influence life and death was as impossible as, as....as to perform magic with your left hand. It was just beyond the bounds of possibility. But on his lap there was this little girl, full of grief. All her life would be grief, tears would never stop falling, day after day. And the tears would rip holes into her until there was nothing left but an empty carcass. He couldn't just watch and do nothing. This child was so innocent!

He took the wand out of his pocket and formed it into the shape of a recumbent eight. At once the girl fell asleep. Some minutes later she would wake up and be able to lead a happy life with a laughing soul. He left the girl in the armchair, in order to have a look at the chaos surrounding them. Using his wand, he reassembled the broken pieces and after a little while the plates were jumping back to their proper places. A chuckle made him turn around. The girl was standing there chuckling at every plate which sprang back to the cupboard, "That's funny!" Mr. Hobbs could not help but smile in return with a certain pride. Faster and faster he made the crockery reorganize itself, while the child was rolling on the floor laughing. "That's soooo funny." When he was finished, she had a hiccough.
"I," hick "I'll have to tell my aunt about this."
"Is this where you live now, with your aunt?"

"Aunt Henriette," hick, "clarinet exactly."
Hihihick.
"What's your name?"
"Sarah. You're funny Mr. Hobbs." Giggling
she hugged him and skipped through the
door.
"Henriette, clarinet. Henriette..." Mr. Hobbs
closed the door behind the child, a smile on
his lips. He was sure he had done
something good.

Years went by. The only thing worth
mentioning was the fact that Mr. Hobbs
was given a cat by Freddo, the fire eater, to
thank him for curing him of his heart
burn. This cat, Mina, loved to snuggle up to
him when he was reading in his armchair.

One Wednesday, exactly ten years, three
months and twelve days after the incident
with Sarah, Mr. Hobbs was sitting in his
armchair, reading. Well, he was not
actually reading, his eyes were trying to
decipher the blurry letters while he but he
dozed off continuously. Lunch had made
him sleepy, and warm sunshine came
through the window. Before he fell asleep
completely, he heard a faint chuckle; it was
probably Mina strolling away.

A slap woke him up, followed by a giggle. Only after a couple of seconds did he feel the pain in his cheek. "Hihi, I woke you up, big wizard." A young woman, maybe 17, was standing in front of him, her hands on her hips. Her blonde ponytail was swinging while she roared with laughter. Somehow it did not sound happy. "Wha...what?" Mr. Hobbs tried to stand up, but then he noticed that he was tied to his armchair. The woman kept laughing, but her eyes were flashing with contempt. Then she turned quiet. "Don't you remember me? To me it seems like yesterday." She stared at him with her green eyes, then she burst out.

"Isn't it funny?" Her laughter died.

"No, it's not! Every day, every minute this goddamn laughter." A giggle interrupted her. When it had stopped, she slapped Mr. Hobbs again.

"This is not funny! Well, here is your punishment, so that you can see what it feels like to be defenceless. By the way the gas tap is open !" The young woman cackled and left the caravan. Mr. Hobbs shook his head. He still had his wand. Sarah had attached it to his left hand with duct tape. Left hand? That meant he had to perform all magic the other way round! Carefully he moved the wand a little to perform a spell to untie himself. With a bang the armchair hit the ceiling. Another try! This time more ropes appeared out of nowhere and started to tie him up. Again! This time the armchair exploded into a thousand pieces that remained motionless in the air. He was struggling with his legs but he stayed a metre above the floor. Think Anthony, think! He tried to tear the tape from his left hand but only more tape wrapped it. The next moment everything banged against the wall, then fell down. He was hit by the arm of the chair. Feeling dizzy, he tried to get up. Further pieces of furniture disappeared or were swallowed by the floor. His hand was shaking uncontrollably. Then he smelled the gas. A spark sprang out of his wand and lit it. In the very last second he was able to perform a spell to slow the explosion down and throw a pot of tea on it.

The liquid entangled the swirling flames, for a moment the elements fought in an equilibrium, then the spell burst and Mr. Hobbs was thrown out of his caravan. Frantically he pulled at the tape. This time he was successful and tossed it away from him. The wand flew through the air, making black and blue sparks, which formed an expanding plasma. With an earsplitting bang this plasma exploded and a blue flame rose into the sky. For a second there was nothing to be seen, then everything was silent. Mr. Hobbs' caravan no longer existed, nor anything that would have given a clue that there had been a home here seconds ago. There was just a gap between the two neighbouring caravans in the field.

The cat was the only living being that saw Mr. Hobbs limping down the road, away from the circus. He became smaller and smaller until he had completely disappeared, like his caravan. The cat yawned, then it strolled to the next caravan to find some milk.

Jakob Möritz

Cisko the Clown

Clowns always wear a smile on their face. They might be frowning, grinning, glaring or gleefully staring at you with contempt. They might be angry, happy, sad or just mad with rage. Whatever their expression, whatever the emotion: They always wear a smile on their face. But what about the audience? Are they always wearing a smile on their face? No. That's what the clown is for, that's why they've come to see him.

Hey kids! I'm Cisko the Clown, and I'm here to make you laugh! Has everyone put on their smiles?

Everybody likes to laugh at the clown who wears his stupid smile. But do they really laugh? Do they just laugh because everybody else does? Do they laugh because social protocol demands that you laugh at the little man with his painted-on smile? It's silly, it's sad, it's stupid, it's sickening. It's anything but funny. But still, everybody laughs. Clowns are a farce. The entire circus is nothing but a fucking farce.

But that's the point. That's what people want. They want to sit back and dwell on the meaningless superficiality. They want to laugh when there is nothing to laugh about. They should be crying.

Hey kids! I'm Cisko the Clown and I'm here to make you cry! Wouldn't that be lovely?

People need to cry more. They suppress the dismal, mundane misery of their shitty lives. They go to the circus to laugh, to distract themselves, when they should be thinking about the sorry world they're living in. People don't need my help to laugh, they laugh at anything and everything just to escape the bleak reality that is their lives. People need help to cry. They need *my* help to cry. But I'm a clown and people don't cry at clowns. They laugh at me because they can't see the true me. Some suspect that there may actually be another me hidden behind the smile they see. They don't like clowns, they mistrust us, think we're creepy. But even they cant see the me that wants to grab their heads and scream: "Open your fucking eyes or I'll tear them out, you worthless piece of shit!" Perhaps that might help them cry.

Hey kids! I'm Cisko the Clown and I'm here to tear your fucking eyes out! Are you crying yet? Good!

Eyes or not, people are blind. No, they choose that blissful blindness, believing it will let them look away. So they look at me and laugh because there is nothing left to laugh about. Would they laugh if I came into their homes? Took their wife and made them look at my knife against her throat? Would it help if I nicked the pale skin on that pretty neck of hers? Let the blood flow, add a little colour to their lives! I would laugh, truly laugh to my hearts content. My face would be smiling and I would be laughing! And the people? They would be crying. I would laugh and they would cry, I'd slit her throat and she would die. Oh my, what a strange and twisted world we live in.

Hey kids! I'm Cisko the Clown and I'm here to make you laugh! And scream and shriek and cry. With joy of course...

Laurence Williams

Tu Semper Mecum

I can hear you. The voice behind the wall. I can hear you whispering through the noise,

I can hear you. If only you spoke in words than I could shout back. But I can't scream into silence. You creep on to me and play on the back of my thoughts, tickling cold nothings into my ears. I feel you when I sleep, lying there next to me. You wait for me to dream of you, for me to run and never wake up. You are the voice behind the wall and I hear you wherever I go. Over the screaming crowds still I hear you. I hear you as I swing, under the lights and above the voices, suspended before the chasm.

Yet even they can't drown you out. I had hoped they would, I had hoped with every ounce of myself that when they called for me, you would be silent. But instead you lift me aloft, you carry me to where their voices cannot reach and it's there that you torment me. My body writhes with your voice, you carry me into heaven, my passion is your chance, my loins your domain. Christ, you make me cringe.

I thank you, though. You led me here, to where the lights blind and the children scream. To the place where reality packed its bags was and abandoned without a second glance. To where I could manipulate gravity, where I could make light follow me as I twist and turn in the air, out of your reach. I feel you all around me, you lift me up but can never touch me. Sometimes I wanted to hold your hand, right at the highest point, I wanted to know the skeletal touch of your affections. And then I would begin to fall. There'd be that tipping point when my soul would settle, harmonious stability in the air before the ground began to grow before me. Your glee as I'd come crashing down was pungent, I could taste it all over.

But I never fell for long, drowning out your disappointment, he would grab my hand and we'd swing together. Tarzan and Jane. I really do have to thank you, it was because of you that we were given this domain, the chance to glide through the sky like Gods. Immortal and unending. It almost seems a shame to watch it burn. Yet, I feel that maybe this was your true intention, you wanted someone, anyone, to make you feel like God. You'd give us a taste of splendour and if we couldn't return it, you'd let us fall crashing back down. Your greed was your undoing and you knew it, you wanted someone to put you out of your misery.

I had considered this long before I stood here. It was never just a thought at the back of my mind; closing the front door behind me the first time I had an inkling. You wanted me, you wanted me to want you and you were going to have me. A spider in the darkness you had spun you web and was pulling me in. I followed your wantings and whispers; you seduced me with your hunger, making me come. Lapping me up you opened up to me, your belly full and bursting with flavour. You wanted to digest me, you would break me down and make me a part of you. I was named the sumptuous fruit and I carried what you had always hoped but never dared to ask, I was the poisonous seed.

I wanted to leave you once. Did you know that? It was the day, you know the one, the first day of the rain, when it just continued to fall. You and I sat there, my hair was in that long ponytail, we sat and listened to the rain hitting the canvas, your canvas. I was thankful for the rain too, that day. My makeup had smudged you see, and the rain provided the best excuse. I had decided it was time to leave. But then.

"Come on, get inside." I looked, and there he stood. I had tried not to look at his muscles, but you saw me, I felt your jealousy even then. It tickled the inside of my legs. His eyes were the deepest brown, so normal, they didn't pierce the darkness nor did they suck in the light. They just were. I wanted to join my moving makeup and fall. Dissolve away into the rain. The more I looked at him the more I crumbled. And then he did the worst thing possible and smiled. Casting a warm shadow over me, Stephen drew closer, he broke the barrier and wrapped his arms around me. As if rain had never even existed we remained there, under your glaring eyes. I felt him guide me to my feet and out of the rain.

"Let's have one last flight together before you decide," he whispered into my ear. I knew that you couldn't hear it. In his embrace I looked up into those eyes, and saw my own smiling back at me. I wish you could've seen it. Oh how I wish you could have felt that warmth, but no you were outside. You had no need for such trifle things, you were far too superior for something so base, something so human. Oh you prophetic fool. Suck my tits, mate. Seriously, right then and there I was truly happy and that made you so damn sick. I melted into Stephen's warmth.

"I think Rebecca has some spare wipes, we can get you sorted out, OK?" I guess that would be it, if I were to fall, I'd have his hand reaching out, and together we would fly. That wouldn't be a bad life I suppose.

"There you are!" I turned to look in the archway, now filled with Rebecca's shape.

"Oi!" Stephen chimed as I turned my head away from where he crouched, wipe in hand.

"Have you heard the news?" Rebecca asked, hurrying to my side.

"You're a hit! The both of you, the circus loves you!"

"Sorry?"

A newspaper was thrown into in my lap. Stephen and I narrowly avoided bumping heads as we looked down. The headline screaming our names so loud it blinded us.

"National paper?" Stephen asked, and as he did I felt his hand glide gently over my cheek, removing any emotional evidence. I looked back up at Rebecca, her face masked in shadow.

"You're the most successful performers this circus has ever had." The smile didn't quite reach her eyes. "There's never been anyone the circus has loved quite like you two!"

"See?" Stephen said, kissing my forehead. I felt Rebecca pull ever further back, pressing against the side of the canvas. "You're a star." He straightened up, taking his scent with him, "Thanks for this, Bex. Hope you don't mind us borrowing your wipes. Makeup can be one hell of a bitch to deal with."

"Nah, it's grand, don't you worry." As she stepped back into the light, I saw Rebecca's eyes twinkling,

"I didn't even know we'd tickled the headlines!"

"Sounds like the newspaper's laughing all right to me," Stephen mused.

I looked back down at the newspaper, devoid of shadow.

"Stephen!" cried a voice from outside. Our ringmaster.

"You're wanted in the ring!"

"Sounds like my call of duty has arrived." We laughed as the man saluted to us and turned on the spot to go. My eyes lingered ever so slightly on him from behind as he walked pertly away. I'm fairly sure you caught this cheeky perversion, I can't imagine why else you'd act out like this. As if I'd forgotten you. I had just gotten up to leave, one galloping gossip chat later, when Rebecca spoke with words that did not belong to her.

"There's something else." I stopped in the doorway,
"Before you go, there's another thing. I'm supposed to give it to you alone." I turned to look at Rebecca but we hadn't lit the lamps and with the setting sun now a grey overcast, her face remained in shadow. "It's a gift." Shyly she turned away and I heard the clink of glass. Her hands caressed the canvas, nails touching the fabric as she turned, the glint of something else in her hand.
"It's a vial of gratitude. For everything you've done in the name of the circus. Consider it the circus' gift." Her hands kissed mine like snow as she dropped the golden edged vial into my hand, the liquid inside nonchalantly leaning against the glittering glass.
You just couldn't let me have my day, could you?

"Where did this come from?" my voice was the quietest it had ever been.

"You made it. Every drop of love and care you put into this place, collected and returned and now it is yours again. You can return to what you once were."

Those were not her words.

"What am I now?"

"Unripe."

Suddenly the room was ablaze with light, Rebecca's eyes dead against the pale white, looking into me with the tender vengeance of a never was.

"Sorry!" Mumbled a voice from above, the spotlight returned to its original position.

"Right!" Rebecca's voice squealed, high and joyous,

"Two hours until the doors open!" And suddenly I could hear them, the first dregs of the crowd outside. How long they had been there was beyond me, but even over the rain I could hear their excitement.

"You'd better be ready, can't let them down now, can you?" I felt the heat of anticipation as she kissed me on the cheek. It burned as I turned to follow her out the archway, and I felt your breath on the back of my neck. The vial growing cold in my hand.

Air pushed down on me and what was left in my lungs began to compress. Being crushed beneath the weight I drowned in the subtle intoxication, waiting for the release. Rooted to the ground, my soul was never to be picked up. I could splutter, scream but nothing could blot it out. You were all around me, you were me, I would forever be a part of you.

"What's that?" His voice snapped me from my reverie. His eyes so kind were just there, a glint of mischief, a spark of excitement that snapped from his to mine. The lack of response drew him closer, his hands touched mine, injecting life back into my touch.

"Bit gothic wouldn't you say?" He looked down at the gift in my hand.

"Tu semper mecum."

"I beg your pardon?"

"It's on the vial. Bit over the top don't you say?" He scooped the vial from my hands,

"I guess they threw it in for good measure, but to be honest it's a bit pretentious." He winked at me,

"But then again, the best things always are." I couldn't control my smile. The man forever with the right words. He took my hand,

"You ready? We're on in a few minutes."

The sky was dark. Hours had passed.

"How old is this?" Stephen mumbled, stepping into the light of the ring. The vial fell from his hands, hitting shadow.

"Never seen you with it before."

"Was just given it." I smiled, reaching down and picking it from the dirt,

"It's a well chosen gift, apparently. From the circus."

"So now the circus is buying you gifts, huh?" Stephen asked,

"Should I be jealous?"

I wanted to laugh.

"You'll feel better after we've performed." Stephen's arm was around my shoulders.

"Do I look that bad?"

"Worse." He grinned, nuzzling into my neck.

"If you think that's bad, you should see me in the mornings."

"Speaking of which, dinner at my place tonight?" My response was cut short by a cry that escaped my mouth before I'd even felt the searing scorch of the vial as it fell from my grasp.

Blood dotted the dirt around the gift as my hand fell open. Stephen was there, a cloth to cover the cut, my hand in his as he slowly wrapped the tourniquet. I felt so distant from the world, watching it in segments as Stephen led me forward, kissing my hand. I flexed my fingers with someone else's strength and marvelled at the warmth he gave me as my energy returned. I failed to even notice that the vial had been grounded underfoot.

"You ready?" I heard him ask through invisible walls, if only then the signs had been clearer. I went to shake my head but instead I felt my neck twist into a nod. Already your grasp was around me. I'd let you in, and I hadn't even noticed. You already had me, what more could you possibly want in this game of games?

How could you forget that day? The day he and I flew the highest we'd ever soared before. The crowd's cries of joy turning to shrieks of horror. Hand in hand we leapt, twisting our bodies around each other. The dance, the practised, repeated dance of the past that had no future. The day you struck forward with vengeance. If I had noticed the vial's cracked glass, I may have reconsidered, but I think somewhere, somehow? I knew this had to happen, I knew you had to act if you wanted me to take you down. And so you did. Up Stephen threw me, and our hands parted as I was lifted high, dancing with the air. At the highest point you called out to me with

Stephen's voice. Tu semper mecum. Oh if only that was true, darling.

I began to fall, it was time to descend. His hand closed around mine and we whipped through the molecules of existence, playing the chords of another man's song. I heard the snap before you even had to say anything, but I saw you laughing in his eyes. His eyes that widened in horror as it became his turn to fall. The spotlight had hit the right spot when it fell from its perch, illuminating the destination. He reached out, desperately but my hand could not be there to grab his own. You held us, one in each hand and then decided to stretch out your arms. And then let him slip through your finger tips. The snapped cable would be marked down in history as the mistake that killed the circus. If only you knew.

I felt his body snap, emanating through my every part. I'd had my fun but now it was time to return to the real world, your world. Of course you remember that day. Your last day.

But like I said, I do have to thank you. You showed me what I was capable of. You made me the girl I am today. This day. Our time. I kicked the bucket and the flames roar to life. I heard your scream come from every audience member's mouth as you writhed in a sea of tides. Oh you fool, you sweet, sweet fool. I was never yours, and now I will just be a number, lost in the masses. The ring of fire, it's a drinking game of death and you have played your last card. So burn, burn my sweet lover. Let's burn together, let them fight to get out, the people who feed you with their laughter, cries and joy. Let them suffocate you with their horror and dread. Let the fear ooze out of every single atom, just one is enough to crush you, small petty little thing that you are. We come to you for entertainment, but you need us to survive.

I think somewhere you forgot that. You wanted me, you called me over, and I thank you, I thank you so much. You took everything but together we can reclaim it. I don't even feel the flames as they change my form. I melt away into the ashes. Breaking free from the constrains of my shape I am lifted, the two of us are. Go on, lift me up one final time, let us fly together, forever, let us fly to the highest point you ever could reach. The point you dreamed of being but never dared. You wanted to dance with me as he could, well come on, shed your shape and dance. I'm sure you'll be front page news.

But know this, you will always be mine.

Monika Pleyer

On this Momentous Night

Madame Raven adjusted the mirror so that it captured the candle light, and smeared the dark paste she used for dramatic effect on her eyelids. Soon her assistant, who she had taken on in Bulgaria ten years before and who she claimed was her own daughter, would open the flap to their shabby little tent to let in the first visitors who were anxious to hear about their fate. Madame Raven made enough money a night to be able to afford a newer, bigger tent, but it seemed that her customers appreciated the tatty crimson tarpaulin and the old, faded velvet that covered her table. Sighing, Madame Raven settled into her armchair. She was getting too old for this, too old to sit in the cold every night. But the circus just wouldn't be the same without her, so she kept opening her tent every night, rearranging the scrying bowl and the glass ball that she had never actually used, pushing it to and fro till it fit her idea of a soothsayer's den, and till it hid from view the scribbled notes she kept on parchment. The tiny sheets were covered in what she claimed was a mysterious, ancient rune system from the Balkans, but which was really a shorthand she had devised with the help of her assistant, who she still did not call by name. On the sheets she had noted down helpful phrases to use when her imagination ran dry after going through the same questions with her customers over and over again.

"*Tonight, you will see a handsome man, who you will fall in love with,*" to say to young ladies; and indeed, most of them fell instantly in love with Carlo, the lion tamer. "*You will have hardships coming towards you, I can see it in the mists,*" to say to the businessmen who hadn't even changed out of their suits. And a general statement, "*You will find your destiny on this momentous night,*" which she used when nothing else would come to her, but which seemed to mystify the customers nonetheless. Secretly, Madame Raven considered this her best invention, adapted slightly from a sermon she had once heard in Frisco. The poor priest would probably turn in his grave – he must be dead by now, presumably – if he heard that his words were being used for some pagan ritual. Madame Raven was chuckling to herself when from outside the tent she heard her assistant call:

"Come in! The mysterious Madame Raven will allow you to glance into your future! Only for the fearless; ten minutes for three dollars; come and follow me!"

Madame Raven had stopped wondering long ago why people reacted to her assistant's claptrap, but since it seemed to do the trick she had stopped trying to get the assistant to change it.

"Come inside, dear friends, my mother will see you soon..." And the veil lifted and there they were, the first customers of the night, a young lad and an equally young lassie, not a day older than sixteen, she with red hair and a slight sunburn, he with an unruly, brown mop of hair and a white shirt a bit too tight. They were probably madly in love, had likely stolen away from home to go and see the circus on what was their first or second date. Madame Raven liked customers like these. They were so easy to satisfy. Just tell them that "true love will last forever" and they'd leave her tent, smiling, and she could see in the girls' eyes that tonight all resistance would cease.

The girl and boy pushed through the veil, and a cold draught came with them. Madame Raven hadn't realized that it was so cool outside, but with darkness often came the sudden drop in temperature that she seemed to forget quite easily nowadays. She pulled her shawl closer to her face and muttered: "Come, children, come, sit down," and pointed at the empty chairs in front of her. The boy came first, pulling out the chair with the fake stuffed raven for his girl. A good choice; she might be able to scare her a bit so that her friendly love message at the end would sink in so much better. She wondered if he'd also buy the girl some popcorn and hold her hand when she got scared at the trapeze act. It had been all over the news some weeks ago. But maybe kids like these were too busy being young to care about the death of a random circus artist; too busy being alive...

Madame Raven realized that both were settled in their armchairs now and were looking at her with bright eyes. She cleared her throat rather loudly. These days she often felt a pressure in her throat that wouldn't go away even when she drank some water. But her mother, whatever gods were out there shall bless her, had had the same problem and had lived to be a good 85 years old.

Waving her hands like she did when she stared into the mists around the scrying bowl she asked:
"Shall I see what the Cup of Life holds in store for you, young lady?" She liked to refer to her bowl as the Cup of Life with women; it evoked images in them of romance novels, marriages, and child-births. But today, even before the girl spoke, the boy said: "I'd rather you used your tarot cards, please,"and, as she didn't react, "it said so on the board outside, ten minutes for three dollars – cards, scrying and runes." "Indeed, dear young sir, indeed. Let me lay out the cards for you and see

what promises they might hold." While she rummaged in the table's secret drawer, she wondered about the choice. Nobody wanted to have the cards read to them nowadays. Everyone went for the mystery, for the glass bowl and the images in there that they could not perceive. Compared to that, cards were boring, and it was more difficult for her to make up a reading without running the risk of evoking things better left forgotten. Madame Raven felt her hands becoming sweaty and folded them in her lap.

If the boy and girl had been the last customers after the show, Madame Raven thought that she'd have turned them away, patted them nicely on the back, maybe offered a crystal gazing for free, and sent them off into the night. Tomorrow, she would have gone on anyway, to another place, another crowd. Who cared, then, about two teenagers dissatisfied with an old fortune teller's service? But Madame Raven didn't want to spoil an evening's earnings and close up the tent under the reproachful glances of her assistant, so she took out the cards which she kept in a velvet box, not daring to admit that her fingers were trembling slightly, and cold drops of sweat formed at her hairline.

As soon as her bare hands touched the cards, she felt a tingling sensation. She could not recall it not being there; the tingling was what she remembered from when her aunt had first given her a set of cards to hold and had told her mother, proudly and a little awed, that her daughter had the gift.

Slowly, deliberately, she began to set out the cards in a pattern familiar to her.
"Is there anything that you would like the cards to answer?" she asked the young boy. But he just shook his head, then, as if on second thoughts, said: "Ask them to tell us our destiny."
"That is a very strong demand, my dear boy," Madame Raven replied, her hand resting over the half-finished layout. "Are you not perhaps more interested in what love might hold in store for you and the lady? Or maybe, you'd like to know about..." but she stopped, seeing that both of them were shaking their heads this time.

Madame Raven realized that something other than her usual pretending was called for. "So be it, then," she whispered. With a swift move that belied her age, she swept up the cards and shuffled. If they were foolish enough to tempt fate, she would deliver. While her hands brushed the cards, she wondered which layout she would use. Not the complicated one she used for love readings, and not the one that looked like a cross. Something different... in the back of her mind, an image formed. She set the pack of cards down and said: "I will read your destiny to you tonight."

The kids huddled closer, the girl gripping the boy's hand. Her hair moved slightly in the draught. Madame Raven planned to remind the assistant to close the tent properly after she had ushered the next customers in; the cold would only distract the customers from the illusions she was creating.

"From this deck, I will only draw four cards." She saw interest spark up in their eyes. Just four cards, that was something different than the intricate layouts they must have known from the movies. "The first card I draw will be your past," she said and laid the first card down in front of her, face down.

"The second one, your present," another card followed and was set to the right of the first, "the third one, what the future may hold." She saw a flicker of annoyance in the boy's eyes, and understood that he had expected more of this than a random past-present-and-future act. The image in the back of her mind burned brighter for a moment, and from the deck she took the fourth card. She felt the tingling grow stronger as she spoke.

"The fourth card I give you is the one that will combine with the three, or change their meaning. It will show you where your true destiny lies, whether you will be lovers or enemies, and whether you will live through this momentous night."

She had scared them now, she could see. The girl clutched the boy's hand tight, and she seemed paler than before. The flickering candles painted strange shadows on her skin that made her look older, worn-out, and for a second Madame Raven was about to call it all off. Not only this reading and these two kids, but the circus, her life as a pretender. But then she felt the tingling again, the devilish tingling, and she set the fourth card down, above the second one, and the pattern was complete.

The wind hushed and the draught stopped. The cloying smell of sage and patchouli that she used to create atmosphere filled the tent. Tonight, it felt more like a living entity, crowding in to get a glimpse of the reading she was about to perform.

Slowly, she turned the first card. On it was a crude image of a human being, half man, half beast, hiding in the dark foliage of an ancient wood.

"This is the King of Beasts. He represents your past. You have not been treated well; people have lied to you, and behaved without mercy." She watched the boy shiver and realized that it was true. Images came to her, of a foster home, of angry male faces and crying women, but she shut them out. Quickly, she turned the second card.

From it, a man smiled up to her. In his hand, he held a rose from which fell a single drop of blood, and a star. Madame Raven paused.

"The second card I give you is the Starbearer. He represents your present. He symbolizes love and desires, but the prize for his pleasure is pain." This time, the girl gave off a quiet sound that could have been a sigh or a stifled scream. A home, seen from the outside, a crying little red-haired girl. A sense of loss and missed chances.

Madame Raven's hands shook as she turned the third card. She only glanced at the image, half-fearing what it might hold. She quickly considered the odds. Two of the Old Ones after the other could have been a streak of bad luck. But three… something was happening, she thought. Even if she had still wanted to call it off now, Madame Raven believed that she might not be allowed to. And a part of her was far too curious to see if the fourth one was what she thought it would be.

"The third one, Celestial, is your future," she said and glanced at the image on the third card. A man's face was barely visible beneath the outline of a distant planet.

"If you leave now, this will be what your future holds: clarity and harmony; the things that hurt you will not hold you back any more." She stared hard at the kids, for they were no more than kids, and said: "Leave now, this is your future!"

From outside, she heard shouting. An angry male voice. A first drunkard maybe, attracted by the sounds and the lights, but she shivered nonetheless. She decided that she would close up for the night after the readings; her assistant could take over. She was as good in the art as Madame Raven.

"Will you accept your future?" she asked the boy. Pale though he was, however, he pointed at the final card that remained face-down on the velvet. "This one. I want to see this one, as well."Though his voice shook, there was a force in it that Madame Raven found unable to resist. She took up the last card, and though she had expected to see the red face of the Demon, she uttered a soft scream.

"This is your destiny." And she thrust the card at the boy. "Death and destruction the Demon will bring. This is what..." she stopped as a shot rang from outside the tent. For a second, it seemed that the world had stopped. Then the screams started. She heard people running, screaming names, children crying. A lone lion roared in the distance.

A second shot rang out. If Madame Raven had believed it a dream, the second sound broke the spell. The kids stared at her, wild-eyed, and she wanted to scream at them to leave, to go through the back door, they might not be seen, but all she said was "Mother Mary."

She could do nothing but watch as the boy tore the girl from her armchair and half rushed her out of the tent when the third shot rang. His shirt turned red all of a sudden, so much like the colour of his girl's hair, and he went down on his knees and fell forward, with the screaming girl next to him.

Madame Raven wanted to scream now, as well, but the tightness in her throat extended all the way to her chest. She tried to swallow, tried to breathe, but no air would come. The last thing she thought about before she was engulfed by darkness was the preacher she had stolen the words from, and she hoped fiercely that she had been included in his prayers on that momentous day.

Jonas D.A. Hock

Little People

The air is hot and humid. The heat from the electric lights carries the steam from the damp overcoats in the crowd and the scent of perfume, soap, caramel, horses and sawdust to the top of the tent. I see the faces turned towards me, glowing with sweat and excitement, people elbowing each other in the sides, children clasping the hands of their mothers. I see my own slender figure standing on the highest platform. I sway a little, dizzy with the heat and excitement. I take a step forward, my naked foot still on the warm metal, then another one into the void. I stretch out my arms and arch my back as I fall. I see my body hurtling towards the ground. I am not afraid. I know that nothing can happen to me. I see myself fall and know that I will not be harmed. I will not shatter on the ground, for the sea of people would rush forward and catch me softly, hold me, keep me safe. My arms are yanked upwards, my legs snap forward and I spin through the air. Marco has grasped my hands firmly and, interlocked, we swing back towards the top of the tent. At the highest point of our flight he releases me and once again I am miraculously weightless, floating in mid air. My body spins forward in a somersault and my hands find the metal bar that is hanging from two long ropes. I glide through the air under the red and blue canvas and, I know that I don't need these ropes to hold me up.

"Carlina, open the door." Taylor banged his fist against the caravan door again.
"Carlina, I know what you're doing!"
The door opened and Marco Fornaio stepped out.
"She doesn't want to see you at the moment Taylor. She says she's tired."
"Tired is she? Don't be ridiculous. You know just as well as me what she is!"
Marco sighed. He closed the door and stood in front of it with his arms crossed. He was much shorter than Taylor and at least ten years older, but he was broad shouldered and his arms were thick from decades of work on the trapeze. "Okay so maybe I do. And what do you want to do about it?"
Taylor bit his lip. "Please, Marco I need your help here. She may not care about putting herself at risk but she must care about you."

Marco laughed, "I'm not sure if I want to think about that boss. I'm sure we'll be fine."

"Well, I don't, so please let me through, Marco"

"Whatever you say," Marco shrugged and walked off towards the other wagons. Taylor knocked on the door again, but stepped inside without waiting for a reaction. The room was dimly lit. Dusk had already fallen outside, and hardly any light came through the lowered shades. Taylor's eyes needed some time to adjust. At first he thought the wagon was empty, but then he saw Carlina lying on a pile of cushions on her bed.

He cleared his throat, "Carlina?" She sat up suddenly as if she had been dozing, "Who's there – what? I – who's there?"

"It's me, Taylor." He stepped towards the bed. "Carlina we need to talk."

She sat up. She was still wearing her tight, silvery white stage costume. Her headpiece had come off and left her hair in disarray and her makeup was smudged.

"Taylor I – I'm really tired. Could we talk in the morning please?"

"I'm afraid we can't," he cleared his throat again, "listen Carlina – you know why I'm here. I don't think you should be performing in your – when you..."

"What do you mean?" suddenly she seemed alert and not at all drowsy anymore. "I put on a great performance tonight Taylor, like I do every night, which is why people come to see the circus. Is that your problem?"

"Carlina don't be ridiculous, you know what this is about."

"Well yes maybe I do" she got out of bed and took a packet of cigarettes from the table "I don't think this is about me, I think this is about you! You don't like me."

She lit a cigarette and began smoking it in short hasty puffs, "You don't like the fact that people come to see me perform – me not you. You don't like the fact that nobody actually applauds you – you're just a glorified usher!"

"Carlina don't be ridiculous. I'm responsible for you and I worry. You could hardly stand when you took your applause tonight."

"I was exhausted! You would know that if you did anything that came close to what I do in the ring."

"Carlina all I'm saying..."

"What? Do you really think we couldn't do the show without you blabbing your mouth off inbetween acts? Without us you're nothing!"

Taylor closed his eyes tightly for a moment, then exhaled audibly, "You're right – why should I care. You just go on like this, we'll see how much good it will do you." He opened the door and left.

Taylor doesn't know me. He is a petty little man. He's not like me or like Marco. He thinks he has us all figured out, but he can only see what may be and doesn't recognize that which is. He is a poor, blind man who thinks I need help. Who thinks that he could help me. Poor poor little Taylor. People like him shouldn't try to understand us. We are different; we are outcasts who the little people admire for a night when we do our tricks. But we are not really wanted, because they know we are different, and they fear that. We breathe fire and swallow swords, we get sawn in half, we tame beasts and we fly. Taylor isn't like that. I know he too hates us – all of us, deep down he can't stand the way we are, because we are different from him and he wants to be like us.

Taylor was standing behind the curtain that separated the entrance to the ring from the audience.
"What do you mean they're not here?" he hissed at the boy who had just tugged his sleeve and whispered his message into his ear. "They are supposed to go on next!"

He glanced through the curtain. The clowns were doing their gags while the next act was supposed to get ready. The Fornaios should be right here, waiting to enter the ring and climb up into the big top for their act. Taylor turned towards the exit to go find Carlina and demand an explanation when they came in, Marco leading Carlina by the hand.

"Where the hell were you? You're on next!"

"Taylor don't start this please. We're here, aren't we?" Carlina replied. Her face was glistening with sweat even though she had just stepped out of the chilly October evening.

She was fumbling with the laces of her costume, but she couldn't fasten them so Marco tied them into a bow while she rocked back and forth on her heels.

"Carlina, are you alright?" Taylor asked. The two clowns had finished their gags. The audience was applauding as they took their bows.

"What? Yes, yes of course"

The clowns came out through the curtain and Carlina turned towards the ring. Taylor held her back. "You two go back out there. Give us five minutes – we need to clear something up before they go on," he turned back to Carlina. "This is ridiculous.

Look at you, you can barely stand still, let alone swing from a trapeze!"

"Oh please Taylor! Yes I am nervous – now please let me through."

"It's okay Taylor," Marco said. "I'll take care."

This isn't right. The faces in the crowd turn into grimaces as we walk past them. They hiss at us, baring their sharp teeth, pushing their tongues out between them. They call me unspeakable names. They say that they will come and slit my throat. They are angry at me because I know. They want their secret to be kept and that is why they say they will kill me. My arms tingle as I'm ascending to the top of the tent; the soles of my feet burn. I look down and I see millions and millions of crawling ants – rubbing their thick, shining, black bodies against each other, clicking their pincers and stretching their antennae towards me. I see their glowing eyes fixed on me and even though I am a thousand miles above them I know that they will crawl up the metal poles of the tent to get to me. I feel a rush of air blowing by my face. I try to hold on but I can't. Why? What is – I feel is a sudden sharp pain. I am enclosed by a darkness, pressing in on me, winding itself around my chest and neck. I try to scream, but no air passes through my troat. I try to move, to run away, but I cannot move my legs. I can hear long, deep, unfamiliar sounds. I don't feel anything, except for the weight on my chest, that is pressing me down.

After a millennium has passed I start to recognize voices in the sounds I can hear. I feel like I'm being pulled up, through the ocean of darkness towards the surface, and as I rise I can make out words.

"– and who knows what else may have happened. I have tried to reason with her Marco, but if she won't accept it, I have no other choice."

"Please Taylor let's talk about this in the morning. Yes I made a mistake, I caught her badly, but we can talk about all this when she's awake again. It's not a problem really!"

"You know very well that it is. You saw her up on that platform, how she was shaking. You remember what happened to that tightrope dancer – do you want that, Marco? Do you want her to end up as a bloody pile of blood and bones in the ring? She didn't jump Marco she fell like a stone. I'm taking you out of the show – both of you. I'm sorry to do this, but you leave me no choice."

Carlina opened her eyes and made a sound somewhere between a cough and a word. Taylor and Marco both fell silent and kneeled down next to the bed.

"Hey Carlina, how do you feel. How is your arm?"

"Don't worry. It wasn't not your fault. I didn't catch you right."

"I think you should lie down again Carlina. We have sent someone to fetch a doctor but until he comes it would probably be best if you lay down and tried to keep your arm still."

Carlina was breathing heavily. She tried to open the drawer on her bedside table but Taylor held her back.

"There's nothing in there anymore Carlina. You'll have to wait for the doctor." She looked at him with wide eyes, still gasping for air. She tried to raise her hand, but the pain in her shoulder threw her down on the bed again. With her left hand she grabbed Taylor's arm. She tried to speak but through her pain her shivering most of the words got lost in a senseless stammer. "Taylor – what?"

Taylor hesitated before he answered.

"Things cannot go on like this any longer, Carlina. I'm – I'm afraid you will have to leave. When we travel on, we won't take you and Marco with us, either you find another circus or try to make it on your own."

Tears were running down her face. Marco got up. Taylor flinched as if he expected the other man to hit him, but Marco just bolted out of the door. They could hear him running through the night, screaming at the top of his lungs. Taylor knelt down beside the bed again and wiped the tears and the smudged makeup off Carlina's face with a handkerchief.

"You're doing this because you hate me," she blurted out through the sobbing and the pain.

He got up "I don't Carlina."

"You hate me! You hate Marco and you hate me because you envy us! I know it – I always knew!"

"No. Carlina, I don't." He crossed the room and opened the door. He turned around and looked at her, lying in bed, crying and struggling for air. Then he left without another word.

Oliver Plaschka

Meditations on an Unsuspecting Assistant

*The day when first I laid my eyes on her –
that very day I lost my heart to her. The
cause, try as I may, I cannot tell – for she
was not the first assistant to our famous
master of the flying knives; and beauty
was a trait not rare amongst the women in
our Circus family.*

*But there was something to be said about
the way she always gave you a brief smile
when she was on her way into the ring, or
how she trained her arms and legs each
day so they would stay as flexible as reeds.
And somehow it called out to me in ways
that I had never once been called before.*

*However, her profession might still be
what made me realize that all of us are
only mortals; and the times we spend
together the most precious gift of all. One
time, I caught her just before her act
arranging knives upon her partner's desk,
then balancing a blade before her face,
much like a serpent charmer pensively*

*attending her beloved and fatal friends;
and when that moment our glances met,
the thought of transcience shadowed both
our eyes – although for reasons maybe not
the same.*

*And when she took her place on that big
wheel clad in her seaweed-coloured sequin
dress, and one by one the lustrous knives
impinged upon the board mere inches
from her skin – how radiant, well-nigh
sparkling she became! An emerald-cross
embellishing a crown, a spinning,
mesmerizing, living sign, but such as one
has never seen in any tomes – a piece of
arcane art created by her placid partner's
steady harper's hands.*

*Or was it not the other way around? Was
it not she who led the deadly dance that
he could barely hope to follow with his
steel staccato on her wooden wheel? Not
for a single second did I doubt that she had
absolute control; and I declared her more
of a magician hence than any master I had
ever met*

.

*Maybe it was this asinine idea, this vain
and foolish thought that she and I were
spiritually linked, even alike, that made me
muster up my courage and approach her*

after her performance and, as soon as she had wiped the makeup and that finest film of sweat off her sweet face, address her in the manner I saw fit:

"H-hi there – O God. I-I mean, sorry for d-disturbing you. It's j-just that I – I thought, actually – m-maybe we c-could g-go get some coffee later on?"

Politely, she bestowed upon me the most courteous smile and swiftly slipped away. And it occurred to me that she must be an even greater sorcerer than I, for she had snatched the gift of speech from me – which is, as anybody will confirm, a wizard's most important tool of trade. And of all wizards, I presumed myself to be no minor poor specimen at all: Had I not been apprentice many years to Kane, the great magician of Des Moines? Had I not worked with many master mages; enchanted thousands, millions with my tricks? Had Bartleby not called me "our last hope", and "wasted on an age of unbelief"? And yet, when I at last ran after her to clarify the apocryphal point, explain my upright purposes to her, the only thing I brought myself to say while standing in the face of love was this:

"H-hi again. J-just checking! You know, I k-keep thinking – m-maybe with milk? I mean – I d-do have some, in c-case you want. Have some m-milk. In your coffee, that is."

In shame I had to hide myself away with all the other artefacts: like me, all underrated, undervalued, all; retreated to my wagon-sanctuary, my realm of unimagined dreams and junk, and brooded long and long on my defeat and drank to my illusions of grandeur. I day-dreamed how one day I'd share with her the spells that I and those that were had stored against the void of wonders; stored for future days more magical than these.

There was the cloak that hides you in plain sight; the trusty rope that hangs from ground to top; the jewel bird that sings with angels' tongues; the floating potion made from fairies' dreams; the wardrobe with two doors, yet three ways out, which Great Lombardo used for his last trick; the chain of silver links no living man, however strong, can ever hope to break; the mirror that shows scenes from long ago – a relic from Atlantis, as some claim; the hat that once belonged to Mr. Hobbs, from which he pulled live elephants, they say.

And with the spirits of Robert-Houdin and wise Govinda Sorcar I communed; and soon we all agreed that our disgrace was quite impossible; unthinkable that such a much esteemed, proficient man, a worker of great miracles like me, should wholly fail at such a petty task as to declare his own and dearest will; so glorious a future as the one I painted for myself and her be doomed thanks to my utmost inability to simply voice its mere idea.

So carried by the wings of new-found hope, the ancient confidence of our art, the promise of new wonders soon revealed – like kisses, one by one, upon her skin – I hurried back to her. Again she smiled politely; and expectantly her eyes were locked with mine; and I could feel our hearts then beat in unison on those frail strings that hold our entire universe in line.

But mocked, thrice-cursed fool that I still am, that ill-starred puppet dancing for the Norns – may each be strangled by her own device – the only words that I could muster were:

"A-all in all, I really like regular c-coffee, you know. M-milk, sugar, who cares. Like, black c-coffee, right. Proper copper coffee pot. Peter Piper, pickles. God. Screw this, I'm outta here."

Jana Gulyás

Sergeant Peter's
perpetual passion

My name is Sergeant Peter
I wish I could move for a meter
My narrow cell
So that directly fell
The man who climbs up there like Cheetah.

I'm most respected in manners
My name's on all company banners
My wife's silky hair
Makes the eyes brightly glare
Of all Suzies, Cathleenas and Hannahs.

I have an apartment of utmost appeal
No wonder the ladies of the house feel
Simply like a star
That's just what they are
See their beautiful paws and I'm right at
their heel.

Yet should you meet me on a less happy
day
I will drive you, you can bet, far away
Clenched teeth and raised fists
A voice that insists
Believe me, my grow I'll make you sway.

You see, I'm the King of the Castle
My great influence reaches far, still
There's one little man
Who control I can't can
And who gives me incredible thrill.

He's usually only my servant
Who, at noon, comes to disturb and
Who gives me my meal:
Seal, beef, pork or veal,
All of which I await, simply fervent.

But I have told him five million times
- And my wife in this matter in with me
chimes -
That on my blank dish
I neither eat fish
Nor cucumber, orange or limes.

This prick doesn't see what I'm saying
In front of me he's always laying
Through the iron bar's gate
Right behind the huge grate
On a silver-blank plate
A gray fish in bad state!
I do hatred create
Want to make for his fate

Right before me here, kneeling, him
praying!

And today he has got his big try-out
From the servant's position to fly out
To the top of the tent
As an artist, he'll spend
All his lifetime – if he doesn't die out.

You know that I'm not without reason
of such beautiful fur in this season
My yellow-striped glow
Gives the audience a show
And it shines to attract and to please
them.

My name is Sergeant Peter
I wish I could move for a meter
My too narrow cell
So that helplessly fell
That delicate artist so sweet, ah!

Marjolijn Storm

Le Soleil et la Lune

She sat between the moon and the sun and looked down. Soon she would jump from one to the other. But not yet. Sitting on the platform in the dark, almost directly underneath the roof of the tent, it was as if for the first time she was really seeing her surroundings for what they were. A circus tent in blue and red, a huge canvas kept in place by two large poles, around which a sun, bright yellow with a smiling face, and a moon, paler, with a round nose and a twinkling eye, were painted. The ring filled with sawdust looked so small from up here, like a pancake. The band with its glittering brass instruments was seated in a niche above the entrance, sealed by a heavy, slightly stained dark blue curtain. And there was the audience, of course, clad in darkness. There was so much space and yet almost no air to breathe.

Don't look down. Never look down. We're up here. They're down there. You're either up here or down there but never in between. And if you are, you're lost. You're as good as dead.

The lights went on, the ringmaster held a short, booming speech and without further ado the first act started. A tiny girl, scantily clad in white and red, jumped out into the ring, riding a large white mare, which was followed by three other horses. She looked so frail that when she started doing headstands and jumping from one horse to the other, the audience gasped. It became clear that she was the special protégée of the ringmaster, who, as he did during every performance, was sitting in the corner next to the entrance. Mr. Arcana was a rather rotund man with dark hair, pince-nez and melancholic eyes, which he could not take off her for even a second. Whenever there was a pause in the clapping, he would encourage the audience, shouting Encore, encore all the time. He was in love with that girl, but that did not prevent him from having her rehearse her act from dawn to dusk, that frail girl, coughing up blood each night and sometimes during the day.

Why start with the moon and fly to the sun? It was bound to go wrong. Hadn't that been Icarus' problem exactly? If he had flown towards the moon, his waxed wings would not have melted and he wouldn't have drowned in the sea. She did not have any wings. Not even that. Ilya wasn't here anymore. If Ilya wasn't there on the trapeze to catch her, as he had always been, she would not make it.

The two clowns were next. One, dressed as a jester, young, athletic, kicked the other one, fat, old, clumsy, into the ring. The Jester's costume was gorgeously red, with yellow and blue inserts and his fool's cap with bells seemed to laugh with every hop he made. The other wore a long shapeless coat and a bowler hat. He was called the Professor. Rumour had it that a long time ago he had actually been a professor, before he ran off to the circus with a girl, who left him shortly afterwards. That would certainly explain why he would visit the library in every town large enough to have one. The act consisted of the Jester ridiculing the Professor in all possible ways, in the course of which the Jester would become more and more agitated; he would dance, he would tiptoe, he would gavotte around the poor maladroit Professor, moving around him as if on the edge of things. Now the audience was laughing, but what would they do if they knew that this wasn't an act at all, that this had been going on for a long time, and would be going on forever, reducing the Professor more and more to a gibbering mess of despair.

His arms, which would catch her, with dark soft hairs all over, his dark brown eyes smiling down at her as he was hanging upside-down holding her firmly, confident, always confident. That was what she needed. That was why it had worked. But now Ilya's arms, eyes and smile were all rotting away in a cemetery in another town, of which she could only remember the name but not what it looked like, and they had moved on. As simple as that.

After the break it was Henry's turn. The lions were sent out first to make the audience gasp, and then he appeared, a Hercules of a man, full of muscles, dark complexion, clad merely in a leather loincloth. He commanded the animals with such confidence and fortitude that they did not dare disobey. There he stood, zealous defender of human strength, death-defying, triumphant. Who would believe that he never looked anyone in the eye and that he had a voice like a child? Who would think that the most innocent remark could reduce him to tears? Who would have thought that Ilya's death hit him nearly as hard as herself.

He had simply fallen. Out of the sky into the sawdust underneath. She saw him fall, he was as helpless as a stone in water. The summoned doctor mumbled something about a heart-attack, but that didn't matter. Even his exit from this world had been perfect – he had landed in the middle of the ring. That, she was sure, was something that she could not manage. Ilya could do many things: conjure up a smile even in desperate moments, hum a tune when put under pressure, reveal loveably crooked teeth when laughing, smell of turf and pine trees.

Don't worry, girl, I'm here. I'm always here.
I'll catch you. I know what you're going to
do even before you know it yourself. I was
born up here, me. As long as I'm up here
with you, it'll be all right. And I'll always be
up here. This is the safest spot in the
world.

Miss Temperance was next, with her glass
music. She always performed dressed as a
winged angel, to match the ethereal
sounds she was producing from her tray
full of wine glasses filled with different
amounts of water. Each night she would
pour water into them, assisted only by a
tuning fork. This would take hours. And
now she was standing there and the first
few tones alone would lure everyone to a
different place, a different atmosphere, as
if the past, the present and the future
were one thing only. It was a fusion of
worlds and thoughts. Like a beacon she
was standing there, only her hands were
moving, swiftly, with such dexterity,
producing wisdom, harmony and peace.
Hard to imagine that she had once
scratched her husband's face so badly
during a row that he had been
unrecognisable even to his closest friends
for weeks. Hard to believe that shouting

abuse at everyone was her second nature, her nature outside the ring.

Was there a world beyond this canvas? Once she had believed in God. At least she thought she had. Maybe it was only a comforting thought to have an omnipresent Ilya around her, in charge of everything. And now? How could a dead person be anything else but dead?

It was a shame the Hermit was not here anymore. She called him the Hermit but in fact he had been a hunger artist. He used to be very famous, but hunger artists fell out of fashion and so he would sit there in his cage, day in day out, and the visitors would just walk by. Only a few days ago, they had found him huddled in a corner, the panther in the cage next to him as alive as he was dead. A skeleton. Forgotten long before his last breath was drawn. It had taken him long enough to die, and in the end he had been barely discernible from the straw he had lain on. Sad. She had rather liked him, even though she didn't know anything about him.

Don't grip the bar too tightly, you'll get a cramp. Just keep your fingers in an arch, but loosely, loosely. Play with the bar, don't force it or it will take its revenge. Treat it as if it were an accessory you don't really need. Let your thumb show you the way, just before you set off, it should point in the right direction.

As she was pushing aside a stray hair tickling her nose, she knew all of a sudden that she would fall. Fall to the ground in what would seem an endlessly long time, the sawdust would be coming nearer and nearer, the surroundings would become merely long, vertical beams of colour, and in that experience she would be united again with Ilya. The impact would break her body, and there would be numbness and pain. The audience would gasp, colleagues cry out, panic would set in and Miss Temperance and Mr Arcana would come rushing to her. Henry's thick hands would check her limbs, then he would shrug and burst into tears. She would be put on a stretcher, and the last thing she would see, with almost broken eyes, would be the curtain closing.

But then they would continue the jolly show, and at the end of it, the horse acrobat, Mr. Arcana, the two clowns, Miss Temperance and Henry would walk into the ring hopping, pirouetting, smiling, laughing, shouting in tune with the brass band. All of them would walk round and round, like spokes on the wheel of fortune. As if dancing with Death itself. Weakness, Dominance, Wickedness, Clumsiness, Strength, Insecurity, Patience and Irateness would turn and turn in an eternal whirl, and Death would be dancing in the middle, spinning the wheel, leading a danse macabre no one could escape from.

To gain thrust you must look. Look wide, take in all the space you have, from this platform to the sun's nose over there. As soon as you have grasped the space with your mind, you want to explore every corner with your body. And you will.

The audience's loud applause and the ringmaster's booming voice woke her out of her thoughts. It would be her turn in a couple of seconds. Automatically, she rose and slid her hands into the bag of magnesium carbonate hanging in a corner. Then the spotlight was turned up and everything was cast into glistening light. She smiled, she was prepared for what was going to come now. Swiftly, she unclipped the trapeze bar from its holder, grabbed it with both hands, adjusted her position, and then pushed herself away from the platform. Three swings later she was flying through the air. How she loved that feeling of the wind rushing past her ears, that joy and elation that took hold of her heart, even if it would be for the last time. When her hands clasped the other bar, the audience clapped politely.

Angela Queisser

That big Scene

... Metro Police say they are following several leads on the case.... Another big event in the city is currently taking place down at Cherry Beach. Almost thirty years after the infamous Circus massacre that shocked residents in the area, the movie "The Last Performance" is being shot at the original scene of the mass murder, reconstructing the event according to eye witness reports of survivors. Not only has the production company recreated the scene using original trailers and other authentic props they bought from collectors, they also found an authentic performer to play the role of the disturbed ringmaster who shot 18 people in the middle of a circus show. The actor who was contracted for the part is his own son, John Stevens. Frank DiMarco went down to the set today to give you an exclusive view of the shoot. Here is what he found.

The news girl's fake smile, flashing with bleached teeth, disappeared from the screen, and was replaced by DiMarco, that idiot. John had never liked that guy when he had seen him on TV, but this morning he had come to hate him. Now the screen showed DiMarco pass through the outskirts of the set, towards the backstage area. As he made his way, he interviewed several crew members.

"Things ain't goin' too well. Been shootin' the same stuff over and over again," one of them explained for the camera. Then, with his jaw clenched and his knuckles white around the remote, John watched as they showed DiMarco approach the make-up trailer, where their little encounter had taken place. He knew the rest of the story. John himself would emerge from the trailer, and try to push past DiMarco. Then DiMarco would ask him what it was like to play his own murderous father, and John would mumble "no comment". Then he would shove the camera away. He decided to spare himself the ordeal. He silenced the TV with a quick waveing of the remote, and then tossed it into the farthest corner of the room.

He was not surprised when a bit later, his cell rang.

"Well, that was awkward," Stella's high-pitched but pleasant voice opened the conversation without any greeting or pleasantries.

"You know that you being the son is the only ace up your sleeve, and it only gets you so far."

"Yeah, I know that." Silence.

"So?" Stella prompted.

"So what?"

"So are you going to pull it together now and do your job right, in order to *not* get fired? 'Cause if you're not, you might as well tell me up front and go find another agent. Someone who's willing to put up with your crap. I *hate* working with amateurs." He could not count the times she had threatened him like that, but now he realized it was getting serious. And he knew she only meant well.

"I'll try, I promise. I already am. It's just... not working out that well." That was a bit of an understatement. He had trouble getting into the role. Scenes had to be shot again and again, until Martin, the director, was somewhat satisfied with the material. On top of that, the press and those B-horror movie groupies had wreaked havoc on the internet, and on the set as well. And John had always been the center of their attention. The 'devil's offspring', tearing the skeleton out of the closet. As for the acting trouble, for a while he had gotten away with acting like it was all too close to home. He had pretended to be doing this as a therapy, to get over all the memories and questions, and all that stuff. The truth was, he did not even remember what had happened, and did not remember his father at all. And he had never really cared either. What he needed was not therapy, but the cash the job meant. But Stella was right. His sob story and the 'prestige' his family connections gave him only got him so far.

"So when are you shooting that big scene?" She interrupted his sulking.

"Tomorrow."

"Don't fuck up."

That big scene was the one he could not afford to mess up. The scene portraying the actual murder. Props would get destroyed, parts of the set demolished, all of it equipment the small B-movie production company could not afford to replace for another take. Thanks for the pressure. The fact that he was not a real actor at all did not help either. John started wishing he had never agreed to do the job, screw the desperately needed money. He grabbed his jacket and stepped out to take a walk. He was not scheduled to shoot until dusk, and as they were doing some indoor shots right now, the outdoor part of the set lay quiet in the light fog.

The only people around seemed to be some crew members on a crane, working on the cables that ran through the trees above. Some of them looked down on him and gave him looks he could not quite identify. He was sure they were connected to the news show earlier, though. Feeling slightly embarrassed, he avoided eye contact and moved on.

It was March and spring came late that year. The trees were still bare and it rained a good deal of the time. Avoiding the puddles that had formed on the main path, he slowly passed the various props they had bought from collectors. Popcorn and candy booths, strength tester, and the like. Some were in good shape, but most of them had acquired a dark patina in people's basements and attics. Most had pieces missing or were broken in some other way, which all added to the edgy look the movie was supposed to have. Looking at the somehow lost and misplaced props, he realized he was in fact one of them. A collector's piece, brought back here for the obsession of authenticity. As he dug into his pockets to find his cigarettes he stopped paying attention to the path and stepped in one of the big puddles. Before he even noticed the cold and wet permeating through his shoe, the world around John went dark.

He could hear faint voices mumbling. He tried to understand the words, but they were too distant. It sounded like thick glass cut him off from them. There was a male voice, occasionally interrupted by a female one. Gradually, they became clearer. The male voice he did not know, but the female voice had that annoying, shrill tone of Stella.

"But can you say how much damage there is, if there is any?" Her demanding, pushy manner was unmistakable.

"I'm sorry Ma'am, but at this stage it's impossible to tell. He was clinically dead for almost three minutes, some people suffer severe brain damage, and some recuperate entirely and fairly quickly. Right now all we can do is wait for the test results." That wishy-washy tattle he had always hated about doctors, that idiot probably did not even know what he was doing. Overwhelmed by a sudden surge of fatigue, John sank back into unconsciousness.

He had been waiting for almost twenty minutes when the taxi the hospital staff had called finally pulled up in front of him. As if it was not enough that he had had to stay in this shit hole for two weeks, now those bastards had made him wait out in the cold on top of it. He ignored the driver as she asked him whether he needed help with his luggage, and simply left it on the curb for her to put in the trunk. He sprawled over the back seat and watched impatiently as the driver took care of his bag. That bitch should hurry the fuck up, she was late already and he wanted to have a decent meal for once before he started shooting. When she finally got in the car, he spat the address at her and then ignored her for the rest of the drive.

He had not been out of the car for more than ten seconds when he heard someone yell his name. It was Martin's voice and it made him cringe. He turned around and saw his director approach with large strides. John's eyes became slits as he watched him.

"So you're good to go?" Martin asked as he stopped in front of John.

"That's what I said." John replied. Was that guy retarded? They had had this conversation just a few hours ago. Martin took a step back, then looked confused and just said "Good" before he turned and went back to where he came from. On his way to the make-up trailer, crew members started giving John that look again.

"What's your fucking problem, assholes?" He yelled at them as he walked by.

The same crap had happened over and over again. The make-up bitch, the fucktard in the costumes trailer, the idiot of a script-guy; everyone seemed to be out to piss him off. Then Martin took forever until he got his shit together and started putting people into their starting positions. First he made sure to give a never-ending talk about how important it was that they would not have to redo any takes. Like people had not gotten it the first time he had said it. Then, after no less than five rounds of rehearsal, he had decided to finally do the take. By then, John was boiling inside. After what seemed like forever, Martin finally called "Action!"

"Let's face it, you're finished! It's time you realized who the real star here is!" The magician yelled at him.

"He's right, your time is up." The clown agreed. That was John's cue. He reached under his shirt and pulled his semiautomatic. He fired two rounds into the magician's face, then one into the clown's. They dropped and landed straight in their position markings. He stomped to the curtain that divided the backstage area from the main tent, yanked it aside, and fired a few more shots at the trapeze artist and the rope dancer who were in the middle of their performance, expecting his entry. The extras playing the audience started screaming and ran for the exits. Chaos broke loose. With the craziest look he could manage, John fired into the crowd randomly as he made his way to the main entrance of the tent. People fell. When his magazine was empty, he pulled the second gun and kept going. Once outside, he fired his last two rounds at some of the scattered extras. Martin's "Cut!" never came.

We have been informed about a dramatic turn in the filming of "The Last Performance" when leading actor John Stevens killed eight members of cast and crew, and hurt 5 others. According to an official police statement, Stevens had exchanged the blanks that were to be used to film the scene of the shooting, which took place 30 years ago, for regular bullets. Witnesses describe Stevens' personality and state of mind as changed after an accident he had on set a few weeks ago. During a break, he had been electrocuted by a broken cable that was dropped on the wet ground he was standing on. Could Stevens have been suffering from the same condition as his father, the original shooter, with his accident somehow causing the disorder to break out? Let's take a look at what Frank DiMarco found out at the crime scene today...

Jasmin Friedrich

Behind the velvet curtain

The ringmaster shouts *Welcome*
elephants are trumpeting
a whip is cracking
popcorn is crunching in their mouths

An old lady screams *Bravo*
lions are roaring
the audience is clapping
children are laughing

Behind the velvet curtain
when everything is silent
it is your voice that is still there